TICK TOCK

TICK TOCK

A NOVEL
BY
GAIL RAMSEY

Sug Books
An Imprint of

The Library of Congress has established a record for this title.
Sug Books ISBN: 0-9748392-0-5

Library of Congress Catalog-in-Publication Data
Library of Congress Control No. 2003099757

FIRST SUG BOOKS EDITION

w w w . g a i l r a m s e y . c o m

This novel is a work of fiction inspired in a very general sense by
women who have loved and murdered. Any references to historical
events; to real people, living or dead; or to real locales are intended
only to give the fiction a setting in reality. Neither the characters nor
the events portrayed should be understood or construed as real.
Rather, they are products of the author's imagination.

Dedication

God bless the one I want to see—
DeAnn Alisa White
1974–2000

My Sister

Acknowledgments

Thank you Mom for *always* being in my corner and for four incredibly gifted, high-spirited, and adoring sisters, Debra, Denise, Donna, and DeAnn, whose love both protects and propels me to feel good, do good, and be good—thank you for the lifts. / To Kevin, Aunt D's sunshine, whom we can count on to say anything and everything. / To Marvin, our quiet storm—please know that when you speak, we hear you. / To Melika, my life and to Malcolm my wonder, thanks for all the high fives. / To my Dad whose way of saying "no problem" has clocked more mileage than any odometer ever could. / To my grandmother Rosalie whose gentle nod of approval would put the best psychologist out of business. / Thank you *number-one* brother-in-law Earl, for always gracing the table, and to Kareema for adding the sweets, and to Ian as well. / And to our newest baby, Charles Dean, who brought us to the moment of joy in the midst of catastrophic pain. / To Doug, who I am so peacock proud to call my brother, *equally so to call my kin*—Nat and Ifanyi.

To the Bowser family, the angel that wears a "K," and the closely woven synergy of friends, thank you. *Hiya Pharr and Lewis!*

Thanks to my best friend, Tweety, *and family*, for sharing so much with me. *I love you Jalia and Adena!* / To no greater friend than Celeste for always hearing me out and pushing me forward in ways that only she can do—Okay, you can remove the hands from the hips now. / To Geraldine Walker for teaching me the magic of listening to Spirit. / To a legal mastermind, girlfriend, and caring spirit all wrapped up in one—Annetta Foster Givhan, thank you. / To Tracey Jenkins, now Winchester, a powerhouse of a personality, who taught me to calendar the deadline.

For assistance along the way, much thanks to Dr. Jerry Cimmet, a psychologist, who has a great imagination and also to the physicians, attorneys, police officers, and the kind people of Bermuda, who helped tighten the loose ends of the book.

Thanks to an unbelievable and supportive cast of characters *for real, for real*, cousins, aunts, uncles, friends of family, co-workers and mo' friends. West coast sunshine—we miss you Risa, you and yours! *Congrats on the Esq.*

I deeply appreciate my editors Lisa Joanis Teman, who helped me with the rough starts, and Susan Malone for penciling me through the art of fiction to the finish line. / To the memory of Professor Sue Rosewalb, whose last class at American University was one of the first that taught me to color the page. / To Professor Diggs-Brown, Professor Richard Stack, and Theresa Spinner whose responses to "Can I run something by you" taught me to evaluate headline news. / A very special *wow* to Sharron Smith, my *undercover* publicist, for the spotlight circling *Tick Tock*. Similarly, thanks to James Paige for your talent and energy on the promotional designs, thanks as well to Jason and Malcolm Brown, keenly artistic twin Ivy League brothers, who provided a few graphics on the web; and to Juliana and Steve at Mangobone for the actual www.gailramsey.com.

I owe a bouquet of fresh-cut lilies to James Rahn of the esteemed Rittenhouse Writers Group for not tossing me out of his class and for challenging me to make *it* better; and to a beautiful, gifted writer and inspiration, Diane McKinney-Whetstone, who said to me—you should do *it!*

To Kelvin—my solid ground. Thank you for the *Island Escapades*.

For allowing me to be—Thank you, God

Gail White Ramsey
Pennsylvania
April 2004

Sug Books
An Imprint of

Chapter One

The whistle had just signaled the start of a rainy Mother's Day race in Philly. My first few steps felt awkward as I struggled to coordinate my arms, feet, and legs into a rhythm.

Someone approached—fast—yelling, "Spiegel? Spiegel Cullen?"

The voice jarred me from my stride. I'd recognize James' voice anywhere, but didn't turn an inch. I'd never been able to talk much while jogging. I nodded when he caught me and thought only of the finish line up ahead, hoping he would dash on by.

Puffy clouds hung in the sky. "I've been trying to reach you," he said.

So what? I thought, but said, "Can we talk later?"

"It's important."

God, that very vain disposition was what earned James Jordan the title of "ex-lover." Such is life—a zigzag dance until we get it right.

I wiggled and jiggled through the openings to find a comfortable lead over some of the slower runners and yelled over my back, "I'll meet you at the end of the race." I panted and sped up to get to the finish line before he did.

"Wait!" he yelled, his tone angry, defiant. "Wait, girl."

I loved it! Ignoring him, I continued without so much as a hint of interest in whatever James had to say. Well, maybe a little interest. "I wish my sister Aliá was here," I murmured. She'd get the scoop.

It was all I could do to keep up with the demands of the whistle that had blown twenty minutes earlier to start the race along the tranquil, muddy Schuylkill waters on West River Drive. The big, green Slippery Elms and Scarlet Oak trees that stake their claim on both sides of the river were in full bloom. People often stopped by to watch the geese entertain anyone willing to feed them fresh popcorn or brown bread. On that day, however, the ducks stayed in the water as a few thousand joggers eased on down the road to raise lots of money to fight breast cancer.

The Mother's Day run, a tradition in our dear City of Brotherly Love, had people racing for a cure either "in memory of" or "in celebration of" various persons. James and I had started running this race together almost ten years ago, in memory of his mother. She had been my mentor in law school when she was diagnosed. Dorothy was so sweet; everyone loved her. How she ever produced a son as screwed up as James was beyond me.

Just the thought of James running somewhere close behind— that he was yelling my name as though he had lost his mind— propelled me to run even faster. What could be so important? We had not spoken since he had suddenly lost his fear of commitment and two months after we'd split married some girl pathetically lurking in the wings. I had heard that they now had a baby on the way.

"Be patient," he would say every time I brought up the subject of marriage and kids. Now there I was, childless, and not necessarily by choice. Mother's Day was not one of my favorite holidays; hell, it wasn't even a holiday. Was it?

I didn't want a baby years ago, so I didn't have one. Today I did, I really did. I no longer cared what motherhood would do to my career. But, if one could believe anything doctors said, my time was almost up in the fertility department. I figured I had eighteen months, nine days, seven hours, eleven minutes, and a few seconds left to fall in love, marry, and give birth. At the rate I was going, even my little sister would beat me to the maternity ward.

As the sunshine attempted to break through the clouds, a bald-headed woman jogged up on my left. We ran together for a while, elbow-to-elbow, knee-to-knee. At least thirty minutes into the race, sweat dripped from my face. Our eyes met briefly. I matched her smile. I would just die if I lost my hair. Shame on me—wasn't it enough to survive cancer?

Approaching the finish line, I saw some familiar faces and many of the runners first out stretched on the wet grass, getting back their electrolytes with orange juice, pretzels, apples, bananas, yogurt. There was no sign of James. But all I could think of was that last cup of water I had downed, because I had to pee. My jogging tights and tee were sweat-soaked. My heartbeat raced, even though I had come to a stop. News trucks and sponsor trucks handing out bottled water and T-shirts lined the sidewalks.

"Hi, Spiegel. Good job. Forty-two minutes," said one of the race coordinators.

"Hey, thanks," I said. I handed him my race ticket, which would officially record me as a woman a few days shy of thirty-seven, who finished the 5-k somewhat slower this year than last year. Forty-two minutes? I would have stopped to chat, but didn't want to take the chance of running into James. That, by now, he was out of breath and frantically trying to catch me, like a dog in heat, gave me joy.

"Well, *excuse* me!" I snarled when this young guy bumped into me, stepping on my clean sneakers without saying a word. But sheer jubilation prevailed among the others who had reached the end of the race. Some of the cancer survivors were talking to news reporters, sharing their stories of triumph over tragedy. I put a little more pep in my step and turned in the direction of my little oasis of a home, or what James used to call *"a geisha haven for you and your too-independent attitude."* Fuck him! James Jordan was an arrogant chauvinist pig, and no, I was not PMS-ing. I just like my space and place nestled in the midst of big green trees and lots of other natural stuff, in the city but close to a jogging path near the river.

In only a few minutes I arrived home and rushed through the front door for the toilet. Then, I opened the windows and let the air and sunshine quietly fill the room. I stripped piece by piece, headed for the bathroom, and stepped into the shower to lather up with a kiwi-scented bath gel, a "just because" gift from Craig. Craig Nicks—my latest attempt to get over James. I wanted the relationship to work like nobody's business to show James that I was really over him.

I rinsed off quickly and pulled a towel around me. In the bedroom, chirping birds outside my window became part of the background while I reached for my favorite soothing lotion. I squeezed a little too hard and juggled to catch the stuff spilling off the edge of my hand. As I spread the lotion over my belly, I wondered what James—I meant Craig—was doing. As an assistant district attorney, I found this sort of downtime so rare that I surrendered to the moment.

I flopped on the bed, fell on my back, and noticed the sparkling mirror clusters that colored my ceiling. The sparkling specks seemed to notice me as well, as I allowed my eyes to roam to what James dubbed his little chocolate chip—a mole on the right side of my cheek. He had a name for almost every part of me. My legs were "Tina Turner legs." I shook my head from side to side.

"What's love got to do, got to do with it?" I began singing, slowly at first, then picked up the pace and belted as if alone in an elevator. I grabbed a Temple Law T-shirt from the pile of clean clothes scattered on my bed and continued my Tina Turner impression. As I stood up and started dancing through my bedroom, I heard, "Spiegel, can I come in?" I couldn't tell if the voice was coming from outside the window or from inside my condo. Had I left the door unlocked in my rush?

"Spiegel, I need to speak with you. It can't wait," James yelled from outside my window.

By now, my café latte complexion no doubt was showing various shades of rage as I contemplated grabbing my pistol and blowing his ass away. Justifiable homicide. I dressed quickly, hollering while bolting toward my front door, "James, get the hell away from here before I . . ."

"Breanna is in trouble," he yelled through the window. "I need to talk with you. She, she may have killed her boyfriend."

"What?" *What?* Did he just say killed her boyfriend?

"Can I come in, Spiegel?"

"What are you saying?" I moved closer to the window, trying to untangle the insanity I had just heard.

"I need your help."

A few good things did come out of my relationship with James, one—my relationship with his younger sister, Breanna. I hadn't seen much of her lately, but she and my sister were closer still—girlfriends.

I opened the door and James stumbled in, still wearing his racing attire. Responding to my cue, he leaned against one of the barstools in my kitchen area. He looked like he had been in a fight with a bear. His curly hair looked unkempt, and he smelled badly too, of underarm funk. His eyes roamed from my head to my toes before settling on my face. He didn't speak right away. He just looked at me cautiously. Shoot. I was only wearing a T-shirt. I tugged at the hem. *It covered enough of me.*

I rushed him with questions. "Where is Breanna? What do you mean she may have killed somebody?" A chilly breeze circulated the room.

He spoke. "They were vacationing last week in Bermuda, and they had a fight."

"Bermuda? Where is she now?" I could hardly keep my thoughts together. "Is Breanna all right?"

"She was scared, Spiegel. She left Bermuda without him." James lowered his gaze to the floor.

"The football player? Did she just up and leave Bermuda?" I had an instant headache and moved about in the kitchen, sitting and then standing, standing and then sitting again. I wrapped my arms around my waist to steady myself. I asked slowly, one word at a time, "Was she arrested?"

"No, and not the football player." His mischievous brown eyes looked up at me. "The police over there want her to return for some sort of preliminary inquiry."

"What the hell happened, James?"

"She left the island before the guy's body washed ashore."

"Washed ashore?" I stopped. "Did he drown?"

He glanced hastily at my bare legs and red polished toenails before answering me, "I don't know."

"Who? What guy?"

"Sean, Sean Thomas. He and Breanna have been going out for maybe two years." He looked me square in the eyes and said, "I never liked the guy."

"Sean," I said quietly, more to myself than to him, while thinking, where was his respect for the dead?

"We're meeting with a lawyer in a few days," he said, glancing at the fireplace. The charred wood and ash from last night's date were still present. He looked up at the customized etching of the *Waiting to Exhale* book cover that hung over the mantle.

"Who?"

"Walter Paine," he said. "Isn't he your friend?" I nodded. "Can you be there, Spiegel?"

"For what? Walter is one of the best lawyers in the country."

"Can you be there—as a friend?" He nervously wiped his brow. "Breanna has not uttered so much as a word since the incident, and I know that she'd speak to you."

I placed my head between my hands to try to stop the room from spinning. I opened my mouth but nothing came out. An intense sensation of heat ran through my blood, prompting all of my vital organs to throb. I can't do this, I thought; I'm not the one. As much as I hated to admit it, I was still in love with James. Anyway, I was a prosecutor, not a defense attorney, so everyone would understand.

"It was an accident, Spiegel," he stated. "Can you come over at least to see her?"

"Now?"

James moved a little closer in my direction and said, "I knew you would be running today. I've tried to call you, but I always got your answering machine."

"Let's not go there," I snapped.

His eyes widened. "I'm sorry. I need your help. I only meant to tell you about Breanna's situation." He backed up out of my face.

Imagine that, the arrogant, indignant, self-centered, inconsiderate Mr. James needed me.

"Are you okay, Spiegel?"

A range of emotions surely showed on my face. Beads of sweat started to collect on my forehead. Hot and weak, I wanted to hit and hug James at the same time but answered, "I'm okay."

He pulled himself from the stool to stretch. "Can I have a glass of water?"

I extended my hand toward the water cooler.

"Thanks, Spiegel. How's your family?"

"This is not a social visit, James," I snapped again, and ripped a hangnail that I'd been playing with for the past ten minutes. With the chiming of my cuckoo clock, I realized that James had been in my company too long. I was ready for him to go. "Why don't you let Walter handle it?" I asked. "He's very good, you know."

"We trust you. And, well, you know . . . Breanna has a temper."

"What do you mean?"

"It was an accident, Spiegel, let's just leave it at that." He moved nervously in a circle.

"James, this is awful."

James moved closer to hug me and I hesitated, but then relaxed into his embrace. He whispered, "Cuckoo, cuckoo. Why doesn't that thing say ding-dong or tick-tock for damn sake?"

The telephone rang, ripping us from the moment.

"James, you'd better go." I backed away to catch the phone.

It was Craig, reminding me that I'd invited him to meet my parents later that evening. "Did I interrupt something?" Craig's voice sounded much as it did when he was anchoring the sports news—upbeat. Most people said he looked like Detective Jones on *NYPD Blue,* tall and brown, except for the red hair. He got upset when people called him carrot top so he kept it cut short, so short he looked bald. His beautiful round almost-bald red head attracted me to him in the first place.

Knowing he would not understand, I lowered my voice and tried to sound cute and sexy. "Something has come up, baby."

"What?"

"I was actually on my way out."

He didn't sound too upset. "To go where?"

"Baby, trust me. I'll catch up with you later tonight."

James watched as I hung up the phone. "Are you seeing someone, Spiegel?"

"Are you married?" There, I had said it!

He looked at me like I had just smacked his face. "Does that mean that you will be there?" He shifted his eyes to the phone. "Do you have a date?"

"Walter can handle your case, but I will call him." Pointing the remote at the TV, I clicked to local news and noticed the most perplexing look on the reporter's face. She was polished, of course, but she looked uncomfortable, as though she were about to blurt out something emotional.

I hit the volume just in time to catch an awkward pronunciation of Breanna Jordan's name. James blinked to release a string of tears, taking a gulp of air as they rolled down his face. *Tears. Damn.*

Breanna, James' little sister, I thought, while looking at the TV screen, then to James, then back to the screen.

A photo of Breanna appeared on the top right of the scene under the caption of breaking news. "Ohmygod . . . Ohmygod!" I said softly. Seeing Breanna's picture on television made everything James had just told me so tragically real.

The news reporter said, "Our top story today, Sunday, May 9th: Breanna Jordan, daughter of Congressman Felix Jordan, is wanted in Bermuda for the murder of her boyfriend. The two were said to be vacationing on the island when the murder was committed. Sources close to the investigation said the congressman had no comment." The news anchor shuffled papers, looked directly at the camera, and said, "Stay with News 10 as this story develops. More in a moment."

I felt both dazed and jolted, when James broke the silence, "You see, Spiegel. We've got trouble."

Chapter Two

James greeted me at the door of his father's home in Germantown, a charming Philadelphia cornerstone. He had cleaned up well and looked strikingly different from a few hours earlier.

"James." I tried to muster a business tone, but made no mistake about it, I was split right down the middle about seeing him again. I was there for Breanna though, to hear what she had to say. He ushered me into a bright and airy home-office to the left of an open staircase. The home was much the same as I'd remembered—warm, conservatively decorated, and smelling of fresh bread or something baking in the oven.

Photos of Felix with everyone from President Bill Clinton to the diva of soul herself, Ms. Aretha Franklin, lined the stairway. Some folks say Felix Jordan, who succeeded his father, was one of the most influential African-American leaders of our time. *Was he worried about his position? What if this was all a conspiracy to bring him down?* As part of his platform, well over twenty years ago, Felix vowed to be tough on environmental polluters. He had deep roots in politics. Even before Congress, he served as foreign policy director for a former governor.

"Can I get you anything?" James asked, smiling. "You look good girl—I've always liked that color on you."

I'd remembered and wore a lime-green fitted cotton button-up blouse to complement a pair of black straight-leg pants and a short, black leather jacket. Also the way he liked it, my hair, even with the two strands of gray, was washed and blow-dried and fell into place in a blunt cut, just above my bra line.

"If you don't mind, James, I'd like to speak with Breanna," I said. He reeked of *Obsession for Men*, my favorite fragrance on him.

"Sure," he said. "She knew that you were coming. Are you going to be her lawyer?" He came up from behind me, close enough to whisper into my ear, "Why don't I take your jacket while you make yourself right at home?"

"You're married, James."

"Why do you always bring that up?" He shook his head, annoyed. His otherwise fair-skinned complexion reddened a little. I turned away.

A large portrait of their mother gave the room an eerie feeling. Her greenish brown eyes and white smile were so bright. She was wearing a scoop-necked white top and a gold love-knot necklace that showed off her peanutbutter color. She was beautiful and her daughter had inherited the same high cheekbones and bouncing dark brown hair with natural auburn highlights.

Breanna appeared at the doorway, wearing a lilac sweat suit with matching socks and no shoes. All of her hair was gone, so to speak. It was cut close to her scalp. She looked twenty pounds thinner and her complexion was pale. Her cheeks were sallow as were her eyes—like a dying patient. I wondered if being there was a smart idea. Was I too close to her, still too close to James?

"Spiegel, thank you," she whispered. She waved for me to follow her to another room, her pants rustling as she walked. She flopped on a large sofa in front of a bay window. The sun's rays appeared to be embracing her, protecting her like a guardian angel. "This is my favorite room—good *feng shui*."

Fung Shway? "Hi, Breanna." I greeted her with a kiss. She hugged me back. She let go abruptly when James ran into the room.

James said, "I spoke with the lawyer, Walter. He's out of town but I have a number for you if you want to call him." His tone was edgy as he handed me a yellow post-it note with Walter's telephone number.

"James, please go," Breanna pleaded, trying to stand up to her brother.

"Are you her lawyer now?" James was getting that crazed look in his eyes. His words were fast, and spit flung in my direction at the end of each word.

"I'm here as a friend, James, but since I *am* an attorney, anything said between Breanna and me is privileged." That may not have been completely accurate but I wanted James to leave. James could lose his temper in a heartbeat, and I relished knowing exactly which of his buttons to push.

He glared at me. "I want to know what Breanna says to you, to anyone for that matter."

"James, either you are going to leave or I am—"

Congressman Jordan leaned into the doorway with a raised brow before he entered the room. He nodded hello as he walked past me to get to James. The scent of liquor preceded him but his voice was authoritative, nonetheless. "We will leave you and Breanna to talk. Come on, James." Felix nudged his son, and then grabbed him by the arm. Felix, still quite good looking with a touch of salt and pepper around the temples, was an older, distinguished version of James.

Breanna shrugged and forced a smile as Felix and James left. "Have you ever been to Bermuda?" she whispered, avoiding my eyes.

"No, not Bermuda."

"I thought . . ." A frown cloned her oval-shaped face.

"You may be thinking of the Bahamas," I said, reading her thoughts. "Aliá and I went to the Bahamas last summer."

I smell banana bread," she said.

"Breanna," I said, trying not to notice how different she looked. Her breasts were much larger than I recalled. She looked to be about a 32-*double D*.

"Implants," she said, as my gaze was not quick enough to shift from the stare.

"How are you feeling?" I asked.

"Am I going to go to jail, Spiegel?" she wanted to know, her gaze darting from left to right and back.

"Breanna, stop it, talk to me." I reached for my pen and pad but changed my mind. "Let's talk, Breanna. Can you tell me what happened?"

"In Bermuda? With Sean?"

What else did she think I was talking about? "Yes. I am going to be honest with you, Breanna. You may be in a whole lot of trouble." I felt nervous for her myself.

"Do you think I will go to jail?" She repeated. "Leaving the scene and all?"

"What the heck happened?" I asked.

"Did you know that I was in law school?"

"No. When? What school?"

"Temple, at night." She looked all of a sudden like a proud rooster, even puffing out her *double-D* cup.

"You gave up journalism?" Breanna had attended one of the top journalism schools in the country on a full scholarship, as I recalled.

"Actually, I wanted to combine my interests—like Ann Rule or Star Jones . . . maybe even work for a network or newspaper, covering the legal beat."

"Sounds like great career strategy." I fumbled in my purse for a cigarette, but then remembered that I had quit. "What happened?"

"Oh . . . I'm still going to do it."

I was confused. "What?" I stood up. "What are you still going to do?"

"Oh . . . Sean?" As her mind zigzagged all over the place, her voice went in and out of whispers.

"Why don't you tell me what happened in Bermuda?"

"O—okay . . . Sean and I needed some time away," she whispered. "That semester had been tough."

"What did you say, Breanna?"

"I was saying, we needed some time to get things back on track. So, I booked a flight to Bermuda."

My throat went dry. "*You* purchased the tickets?" I sat down and cleared my throat.

"Yeah. . . . At first, Sean didn't even *wanna go*," she said swaying her neck. "But later Sean called and asked, 'When do we leave?' I was so happy to be done with the semester. My mom would have been so proud of me." She paused. "Do you like my haircut?" She went over to the mirror and played with what was left of her hair.

"The cut looks cute on you."

"My mom had the same cut—do you remember?"

I couldn't answer. I don't know why. I'd remembered her mother had lost her hair from chemotherapy. She looked so much like her mother it was like seeing a ghost. With the portrait in the one room and Breanna in here, the house seemed haunted.

"She never told me that she was dying," Breanna said.

Not so many years ago, Breanna's life had changed in a way that no fifteen-year-old girl's ever should. She spoke straight ahead into the mirror. "I didn't know my mom was so sick." She suddenly started to cry; her face held only pain. Then her voice dropped back down to a hush. I didn't move, couldn't, but shared her pained expression.

That rainy Monday almost eleven years ago, we had laid her mother to rest. James stood by his sister's side, holding her up. Breanna had crumbled into a weakness that only death could bring forth.

"You were there, remember?" She pivoted from the mirror to face me.

"I remember." Breanna had never made it to the burial site. My own mom put her to bed after the doctor gave her a sedative. Aliá and I waited at her bedside practically all night before she woke again, calling for her mother.

"How long had you and Sean been dating?" I tried to get her to focus.

"Oh, he will be back," she said.

I paused. "What do you mean, Breanna?"

"Three years," she answered slowly, almost with a jazz-singer's tone, "three long years." She smiled as she exaggerated her words.

"Did you say three years?"

"Yep," she stated. "He'll be back; we've done this before. He was engaged when we met, ya' know. He broke it off with his fiancée, though." She looked up at me for some sort of response. None came. Had James and Felix kept the girl secluded in this house and never told her that Sean, well, wouldn't be coming back?

"Breanna, come sit next to me."

She sat down next to me and continued, "A trip to the island, I thought, would be good for us, you know. He had been working so hard and always seemed so tired."

"Breanna, pull it together." I had studied her closely, but saw no signs of real grief, not even sadness about Sean until now.

A tear fell. "Do you know if he was hurt bad? Have you heard? No one seems to know."

No one had told her that Sean was dead? "Breanna, you have to pull it together."

"I . . . I, was scared." She moaned, pulled her legs up to her chest, and wrapped her arms around them rocking back and forth. Her words became fast and chopped. I got up to get her father, but then thought better of it when I saw her groping frantically around in an overnight bag. She pulled out a small bottle of pills.

"What is that?" I asked.

"Something my dad's doctor gave me for cramps. It's that time of the month, you know." After she took the medicine, she sat quietly for a few minutes and became unbelievably calm.

"Breanna, can you tell me what happened?"

"Well, we arrived in Bermuda on Friday. There was a van waiting to take us to this hotel called Sonesta—girl, the hotel was all'dat! Right on this beach—bunch of wealthy folks! We got a good package from my dad's travel agent, the Distinct Destinations lady." She smiled. "Anyway, we dropped our bags as soon as we got there, rented a moped, and went sightseeing. Sean had to hop on the bike with me since it was his first time in Bermuda and his first time on a moped."

Breanna stretched her otherwise skinny body out on the sofa. Lying on her stomach she propped herself up on her elbows and continued, "Our last stop was Fantasy Cave. It was so captivating."

"After the tour, we went back to the room, pigged out on hot wings and ginger beer with rum—a drink they call 'dark and stormy'—and fell asleep."

"We woke up later that evening and decided to spend the evening on the beach watching the moonlight shimmy on the ocean." She paused, and took a long deep breath. "Do you want me to tell you what we did?" She became fidgety and smiled a shy smile. "Talking to you is like talking to a mother. Are you sure you want to know?"

"You can talk to me, Breanna." I was flushed, but pressed forward anyway. "You need to tell me exactly what happened."

"We rode the moped to the beach." She giggled. "Sean pulled some smokes from his sock." She hesitated. "Anyway, he fired it up. I took a drag and stretched out on the sand. The night was cool, but I was so hot inside. Sean pulled me over onto his body, molding us together . . ." She stopped. "Do you want me to go on?"

"Yes, Breanna."

"I was a little apprehensive at first, *ya' know*, on the beach and all, but seeing Sean pulsating once he'd dropped his pants made me forget all about any uneasy feelings. He pulled me right up to the mouth of the ocean. *Ahhh.* I'm getting goose bumps thinking of him." She hesitated. "Spiegel . . . you promise not to tell anyone what we're talking about?"

I was getting goose bumps too and actually wanted to hear more so I said, "I won't be specific."

"You won't tell my dad."

"No."

"Everything—the ocean, the twinkling stars, the dark sky—stood still." She blushed. "He had my legs open for so long I thought I saw the moon smile."

"Did you leave then?"

Out of the blue, James popped his head in the door before she got a chance to answer. "Would you like some lunch, some fresh-baked banana bread?" His tone was civil.

"No." Breanna's smile became a frown. "James, we are still talking."

"Sure. Okay." He backed out the door.

Breanna went to the sliding doors to peek through the crack to make sure James had completely gone. She ran back over to the couch like a little kid with something very special to tell a best friend.

"Girl," she continued with the biggest smile, "we tried to dress but I was so *on*." Her smiled eased as she told me Sean pulled out and his stuff shot out all over her face. " 'What is wrong with you?' I asked him. He mumbled something about not thinking."

Breanna sat silently on the sofa, playing with her hands, before she continued, "Sean jumped up and said, 'It's like, Breanna, I love you, baby, but I owe it to Fay to try to make it work.' It was like someone else was talking, not the Sean that I had just fucked until the sun damn near came up. Fay was that fiancée I told you about. I tried to reason with him because I knew that he loved me and not her, but all he kept saying was, 'I'm sorry baby, I don't want to hurt you.'" She sighed deeply. "But it was too late."

"I smacked him so hard I thought I'd broken my finger, then jumped on the bike so fast that I fell at first, and struggled to get it going. He came toward me. Without thinking, I sped off. I hit him. I know it. Then I drove like crazy back to the hotel."

"Did he strike you, Breanna? Were you afraid of him?" I was thinking ahead, perhaps prematurely, of a case of self-defense—to no avail.

"Heck no! I was pissed. And, besides Sean's a lover, not a fighter." She stopped. "When he never came back to the room. I called my dad, and he told me to come home without a word to anyone. So that next morning, I boarded the plane back to Philly without Sean. I hope he's okay. He hasn't called, and I'm not going to call him."

"Breanna," I said. "Didn't anyone tell you? Sean is dead." I wished I could have taken the words back as soon as they left my lips.

She hurled into me, yelling at the top of her breath, "What are you talking about?" She twirled around in circles declaring, "No, no, no!"

"James! Mr. Felix!" I screamed. I was unable to calm Breanna. Her eyes rolled to the top of her head, she charged straight into a closed window then collapsed, unconscious, on the living room floor.

James and Felix ran in and tried to wake Breanna. James ran out to get the car while Felix bundled her in his arms. Felix commanded, "Call the hospital! Let them know we're coming." I just stood there. "Now!" he yelled.

I frantically searched for the telephone, finally spotting it on the coffee table on top of a spread of little *Jet* magazines.

"And get Walter on the telephone . . . tell him to get back here now!"

"911's on the line," I said.

"Forget 911, call Chestnut Hill Hospital emergency!" Felix yelped as he raced out the door.

I stood in the middle of the room staring at the window after they had gone. A few minutes later, I followed.

Chapter Three

By the time I arrived at the hospital, Breanna had been heavily sedated. *Now what?* I left and called Walter. "Walter Paine, please . . . this is Spiegel Cullen."

"Ah—yes. Ms. Cullen." Walter's voice was deep and pleasant.

"Walter," I replied, opening my car door and settling in behind the wheel of my aging navy Volvo coupe. The breeze of May blew through the well-manicured lawns of the hospital courtyard.

"I assume you know by now that Felix's daughter may be connected to the murder in Bermuda," he said.

"I know."

"Hey," Walter said, "congratulations on the Stewart conviction."

I was flattered that he even knew about the case. Walter was considered by far one of the most-revered criminal lawyers in the state. Having represented a long list of high-profile clients, he last year added to his claim to fame the representation of one of the four guys charged with murder on some small exotic island. His client walked; the other guys were not so lucky.

He was direct. "I want you on this case, Spiegel."

My usually quick comeback was gone, but I managed to say, "I am here now with Breanna."

"Oh?"

"Her brother asked me to come speak with her."

"You could make some real bread should you dare come to my side of the courtroom," Walter said.

"Defend them? I don't think so."

"Not even in this case?" Walter asked. "We are talking about Breanna Jordan. I want you in on this, Spiegel. I know how close you are to the family, and you know that I've been trying to get you to work for me."

Surely, Walter knew that this was not my line of work. "Actually, Felix wants you here now," I said.

"I got the message." A siren from an emergency vehicle drowned out our conversation. "Where are you? Can you hold one second? I have to take another call."

While waiting for Walter to return to the line, I closed my car door and pulled away. I could do nothing for Breanna at the hospital.

Pulling in front of Borders, a chic bookstore on Germantown Avenue, I planned to run in and get my mother a gift, when Walter clicked back on. "Spiegel, that was Felix on the other line." He paused. "I am on my way into the office and will set something up for later today. Are you available?"

"Walter, I . . ." How could I tell Walter that I couldn't work with James? "Walter, this is too important for a novice. I mean my specialty is criminal prosecution. And, besides—"

"This is a chance of a lifetime—you know that, don't you? I'm putting it in your lap." He paused. "Listen, your skills in the courtroom are among the best I've seen. And, the fact that you know the prosecution side is a plus."

Walter was just trying to boost my confidence to answer yes, but all I could say was, "Um, uh. . . ." Why was he really putting this case in my lap? Was it too risky for him to take a fall?

"We would be a team. I would advise you on every detail."
Silence. "You'll never get this action where you are now. Are you
interested?"

"I care about her, Walter." My eyes welled up just thinking
about Breanna's reaction when I told her Sean was dead.

"As quiet as it is kept," he said, "two other bodies washed ashore
last year under similar circumstances." He cleared his throat.

"Really?" My cell phone chimed. I let it ring.

"But, our guy may have hit his head because, from what I
know, there were rock samples sent to a lab in Britain used
regularly by Scotland Yard."

Scotland Yard? Britain? "This is out of my league. I don't know
squat about situations in foreign countries."

"But I do. Like I said, you'll be part of a team and trust me at
some point—it all comes down to an argument of pros and
cons." We were both quiet for a moment. "The reality is that the
judicial systems here and abroad are not that different. Both
follow common law." He paused again. "It doesn't look good and
I don't have to tell you that the congressman is deeply concerned.
Have you spoken to Breanna?"

"Yes." I again thought of the way she had hurled herself at the
window.

"How is she?"

"Not good."

"Will you consider my offer?"

"Okay." Could I win James' heart again? Could we pick up
where we left off? Did someone say wife—hello? In that instant,
though, I knew I would quit my job and accept another.

I strolled through the oak doors at Borders. This was turning
out to be the wildest Mother's Day ever.

After picking out a gift for my mom, I sat and stared out the
coffee bar window thinking of the time Breanna almost poked
out a girl's eye because she called her "light bright." Frankly, her
temper scared me. I pulled out a yellow pad and jotted down a

series of questions to cover at the meeting, starting with: Where was the body found? What time? What was the condition of the body? Autopsy Report? Defense?

I took Germantown Avenue to Lincoln Drive to Walter's office in center city. Despite the early evening hour, the streets were busy. The twenty-minute trip took me a half-hour. I barely missed hitting a red Corvette convertible when I pulled into the parking garage—James' car was parked crooked.

"James! Most people park between the lines," I tooted when I caught up with him and Felix waiting at the elevator banks of Walter's well-known criminal defense firm.

"Sorry," he said, sarcastically.

"Hello, Felix." I kissed his cheek. His eyes were red and swollen as if he were having an allergic reaction to this whole mess. "How is Breanna?" I asked.

"We'll talk inside," he said. We stepped into the elevator.

As the mirrored elevator doors slowly closed, I was startled to hear heels clicking on the marble floors of the lobby and a determined, yet familiar, declaration to hold the elevator. James hit the button just in time to let Aliá in, and I hit the button long enough to escort her back out of the elevator and gesture to James and Felix that I would join them in a moment.

"Spi," Aliá asked, almost at the tip of her voice, "what *is* going on?"

"Calm down," I quietly said. My little sister was known for her hysterics. "How did you get here?"

"I drove. I've been trying to reach you all night. I called James and he told me what happened and that you'd be here with him. I saw Brea on television. Did Brea kill Sean? He was a dog. What has she done?"

"What?" I raised my eyebrows.

"Sorry, Spi. I mean, he was no good for her."

"Did you know Sean?" I brushed Aliá's thick hair from her eyes gently. Aliá was stunning. She had the best features of both of our parents—flawless honey complexion from our dad; long, thick, brown hair from my mom.

"Yeah." Her voice started to shake now. "Sean and Brea have been on and off ever since they started dating. He told her that he was single—that was the first lie he told. She should have dumped his ass."

"She continued to see him?" The two of us stood in the lobby whispering.

"Yeah. It was a bad relationship. Where is Brea? I called her house today, but no answer." Aliá's big brown eyes started to tear.

I hugged my sister. "Why don't you go over to Mommy's, and I'll catch up with you later."

My mother was probably a nervous wreck by now, and her Liá would be of some comfort. She was no doubt at home preparing tofu turkey with loads of vegetables for our Mother's Day dinner. My mom swears that vegetables, especially wheat grass, can keep you cancer-free. One whiff of the stuff sends me to puking.

"Okay Sis." Aliá kissed me and left, still visibly shaken.

"Be careful Aliá."

Both Aliá and Breanna had worked as models as undergraduates, not because they needed the money, but because they loved the attention. They got plenty of it together. Both were a perfect size six with little bubble butts and two-inch waistlines.

Riding the elevator up to Walter's office, I thought of how I had heard from Breanna less and less after James had chickened out on me. Her love for her brother and my disdain for him obviously placed a wedge in our friendship. Did James ever think about me?

Since seeing him again, I couldn't stop thinking of him. By the time the elevator arrived on the fifty-second floor, my delicate daydream was over.

Walter, Felix, and James sat comfortably at a small conference table in Walter's office. My entire condo could fit into Walter's huge office. It had an unobstructed view of the Delaware River straight through to the New Jersey side where the dome-shaped aquarium sat dockside. Walter's office building was one of the first erected in the city that was allowed to go higher than the statue of the Honorable William Penn atop City Hall. Open and airy, yet the dark cherry wood furnishings spoke to Walter's very conservative side.

"I am glad that you could join us, Spiegel," Walter said. A small husky man, always well dressed and manicured, he had most of his suits custom-made and wore only black. "Have you spoken to Jay?" Jay Stanley was the district attorney for Philadelphia, my boss.

I took the seat next to Walter. "Unofficially." Pulling my chair up to the table next to Walter, I said, "I have to make it official tomorrow."

Walter smiled.

"Breanna cannot go to jail." Felix's speech was slurred. "She was scared for her life."

"She didn't do anything wrong," James said with an attitude twice his size. He was quick to step up to anyone. I loved that about him. If a guy ever had looked at me the wrong way, James was in his face.

Walter placed his elbows on the conference table, sat on the edge of his chair and looked at Felix. "Where is she now?"

"At the hospital." Felix put his close-cropped head down. "She'll be there for a few days." He looked up. "They want her to see a shrink."

Walter rolled his chair closer to pat Felix on the back. "Hang in there, my man. Do we know if there were any witnesses?" Walter asked.

"In Bermuda?" Felix asked and rubbed his temples.

Walter cocked his head to the side and nodded.

"The lawyer in Bermuda has an investigator checking that out," Felix said, and continued, "What if there are no witnesses?"

Walter got up and pulled down the wet bar to offer us something to drink. His bar was stocked with everything from beer to vodka. "What do you want me to do, Felix?" Walter asked. "Who is this lawyer in Bermuda?"

"The guy in Bermuda told me that Breanna would have to go back to Bermuda next week to answer some questions." He spoke louder, "Not a chance."

"Do you know him personally?"

Felix shook his head. "He was recommended by a colleague. He is supposed to be a real Perry Mason when it comes to getting Americans out of trouble on the island."

"I've heard that as well." Walter said. He mixed a juice and vodka with a little ice and handed the drink to Felix. Felix's eyes were red and his hand shook when he accepted the vodka. "We *will* need local counsel, Felix. I'll talk with this guy tomorrow. Has Breanna spoken to any . . ."

"No," Felix answered.

"Good."

"She just cries and sleeps," Felix said. "I'm not sending her back to Bermuda, and I don't care what they do."

"Felix," Walter began, "They'll start yelling conspiracy to prevent the course of justice if we don't at least appear to cooperate."

"I don't give a flying fuck what they yell. If they don't know who I am they will find out." Felix stood up. "It was an accident."

"We will see this thing out, Felix. But we have to cooperate."

Felix shook his head. "I am her father." He pointed a finger at Walter. "I'm not just going to turn her over." Oh, no. He can't protect her now.

"Calm down, my man." Walter said.

James looked so vulnerable. Behind that tough exterior *I* knew when he was scared. He refilled his father's drink and poured himself a glass of 7-up. James was married, I quietly reminded myself; but he was my first love. When I made love to James, I made love for the first time. *Get a grip, girl! You have a man. Craig.*

"You know . . ." Felix continued. "Bermuda's tourist industry is second behind international business in terms of economic importance to the island." He paused. "I could compromise them both." He turned to Walter with a raised eyebrow.

I focused and said, "Everything you do will be suspect, especially if you continue to be involved in foreign affairs involving Bermuda. The United States has an image of justice to protect as well."

Walter spoke up. "I am going to see exactly what Bermuda wants us to do," he said. "In the meantime, sit tight."

"Sit tight, my ass." Felix was practically trembling. "Stupid . . . I don't understand how Breanna could be so stupid. I raised her better." He leaned on the table to balance himself. "I know how things work in Bermuda."

The air in the room held a haze of confusion. No one said a word. James stared out at the Ben Franklin bridge, Walter took notes, and Felix swallowed hard. A chill crawled down my back as I watched James.

"Isn't Congress about to recess anyway?" I asked.

"July, for the summer."

Walter sat back in his chair and got down to business. "Well, in most places, if someone pushes a man in the water who subsequently drowns, he would be guilty of a homicide which simply means a killing of another." He paused. "Of course, homicide can take on various categories—intentionally or otherwise and, depending on the evidence, we may be looking at a murder charge in the worst-case scenario, homicide by accident, or perhaps manslaughter. The distinguishing factor is, of course, if the act involved malice aforethought."

"A what?" James asked and frowned at Walter.

"Was it premeditated?" Walter clarified, enunciating with his hands.

Everyone sat silently for a second.

Walter sat up. "The only thing we have to prove with an accident defense is that she had no motive, no prior thoughts of doing away with the guy." Silence. "The weakest link we'd have to firm up is that she meant Sean no real harm," Walter looked at me. "Agreed?"

"Agreed."

"I'd like to keep this as quiet as possible," Felix said. James gulped the corner of his drink and moved closer to his father. "The government over there will want to move fast to restore a sense of safety on their beaches." In a matter of an hour, Felix had gone from stumbling in an emotional downfall to an intellect rising to the fight.

"I'd like to know more about Sean Thomas." I wrapped up my notes and made sure I'd covered all of my questions before preparing to leave. "Maybe talk to some of his friends, maybe even attend his funeral."

"What?" James yelled.

"Do you know when it is?" Walter asked.

I shook my head. "No, but I would imagine sometime soon."

Felix and James looked at me cautiously.

"Do you think that would be a good idea?" James asked. "Would that be safe?"

"No one would know me there, James." Why did he care?

"Spiegel, I agree with James. That may not be wise," Felix said. "Let Walter talk with Bermuda and get a handle on what they're after."

Touched by their concerns, I simply responded, "Sure."

Chapter Four

By the end of the week, I had moved from a windowless cubbyhole at the district attorney's office to a spacious office at Ross and Paine, and had decided to attend the funeral service of Sean Thomas at seven o'clock on Friday evening.

Curiosity, more than anything, motivated me to visit Red Rock Baptist Church to pay my respects. What sort of a man could bring Breanna to such a sad state of affairs? The ushers handed out copies of the obituary as people walked into the church. The family was already seated. I accepted a copy of the handout and looked for a seat.

I sat down and read the words underneath a photo of a nice-looking brown-faced man with a big smile. *"In Loving Devotion and Lasting Memory of Sean Milton Thomas."*

The services began. A short, frumpy, older gentleman walked to the front of the church, stood at the altar, and began to speak. "My name is Clyde Thomas," he said. "Sean was my nephew." A few more people filled the rows in the back of the church.

"My nephew was born on May 1, 1968, to Edith and Sean Thomas, Sr., in Baton Rouge, Louisiana." The man gestured toward the parents and continued, "He attended public school and the Community College of Philadelphia." He stopped and then added, "Or so Sean said."

His added comment was puzzling, almost sarcastic. Because jotting down notes on a legal pad obviously would have been in poor taste, I made a mental note to follow up with the uncle.

I spotted who I thought were Sean's parents sitting in the first row. People systematically went over to kiss and comfort Sean's mother. Younger adults and a few children filled the first two rows.

The uncle's voice was starting to quiver just a bit, but he remained strong as he continued, "Sean had everything to live for. He had recently won first place in the premier body-building contest and was engaged to be married in the fall to his beautiful high school sweetheart and fiancée, Fay, and together they were the proud parents of a beautiful son."

I had heard that Fay and Sean had been together since she was fourteen—some fifteen years—but I had not heard about a kid. One of the local papers even featured a story about Sean with a photo of him and Fay. If I were Fay, I may not have even bothered to show up at his funeral after learning that Sean was dating someone else while engaged to her. I'd want to kill him all over again.

I tried to pick her out. I was sure that she was present, but trying to find Fay was like searching for the legal equivalent of the smoking gun. Many women were present, and it was hard to tell who was special, as they all seemed to be mourning a beloved.

The uncle at the podium voice turned sincere. The hint of sarcasm was gone. "Sean, as we all know, had a flair for clothes and charm, which allowed him to mingle with people from all walks of life. He was very kind and had a real heart for anyone in need or trouble. He did what he could to help anybody." His voice cracked but he recovered. "His favorite day was Monday, but only during the football season." An uneasy rush of laughter spilled through the pews. "Sports were always part of Sean's life—he was a die-hard fan of the Philadelphia Eagles, a fan undaunted by the downturn in the winning streaks. 'Give it your best' was his motto."

"He leaves his love for sports with many of the Little League football players he coached at the playground near the home where he grew up. Sean would be happy to see so many of the little players here today. Yes," he said painstakingly, "Sean is smiling today because you are all here." As the uncle's voice choked, this time with grief, the pastor stepped to his side and read the last paragraph of the obituary, which mentioned a host of loved ones left to mourn Sean's death.

"Precious Lord," the short, silver-haired pastor began, with the chiming in of a soft organ. "Take my hand, lead me on, help me stand . . . Hold my hand lest I fall . . . Take my hand, Precious Lord, lead me on . . . "

The church had completely filled to standing room only. Apparently, Sean Thomas was well-liked.

After the reading of the obituary, some brief personal remarks were made by two young men, friends of Sean. The first was a soft-spoken man of very few words. The other, a really tall guy, practically ran to the podium. His words were quick, harsh.

"I promise you this, Mrs. Thomas," he began. "I will not rest until the woman responsible for Sean's death is punished. We will not sit silently by and let her go free." He shifted his tall frame. "Judgment day is coming," he said. "It is just a matter of time."

"Amen," went up from the pews.

These people had already convicted Breanna. Perhaps my being present was not such a bright idea. But I felt compelled to come, an obligation to my client, to learn about the catalyst that had changed her life. The guy's remarks were heartfelt.

I swiftly surveyed the church for the quickest way out that would not draw attention to me, when an usher appeared at the side of the pew, indicating it was time for those seated in my row to view the body before they closed the casket. *Breathe! Breathe!*

We walked single file, zombie-like. Sean was a tall man. The casket was very long and filled with hand-made cards and drawings; one in particular with an "I love you Uncle Sean" message caught my eye. I should have listened to Walter and stayed home.

Sean was dressed in a tailored navy suit, white shirt, and navy tie. Had I not known better, I would have thought he was a dead lawyer instead of a parking lot attendant. I was a little embarrassed as I viewed the body and thought of how unequally yoked he and Breanna appeared to be. She was a journalist from a prominent family, and Sean had a high school education, some college, but a minimum-wage job. It didn't appear that anyone in this congregation even knew that Sean had another life with a girl who was taking the world by its tail, a girl who could have had absolutely any guy she wanted—except this one.

His once-handsome face was heavily made up. It looked almost caked on but the swollenness above his right eye was apparent. At Sean's fingertips was a colorful photograph of him and a woman. The fiancée, I presumed. I tried to get a good look at the photo but some people were standing behind me, waiting for me to move on, and the last thing I wanted to do was draw attention. I nervously made the sign of the cross and moved quickly as a saxophonist's rendition of "Amazing Grace" filled the church over the crying, the wailing, and the moaning.

As I found my seat again, a plump lady a few rows back pointed at me while whispering in the ear of the police officer sitting next to her. Or at least I thought she was pointing at me. I wished Aliá had come with me. I felt vulnerable. Are they talking about me, or was I just being paranoid? Paranoid, I concluded, and sat back down in my seat, trying to ignore the unexpected appearance of a few ants that were moving across the wooden pew. I brushed them to the floor discreetly with a paper fan and sat up straight to watch as Reverend Reid, the pastor, again stepped forward to talk over the saxophonist's notes.

"If there was ever a family that needs your prayers, it is this family," said the reverend. He wiped the sweat from his forehead and paused for a moment for effect. "We heard the talk; we have our suspicions that Sean's death may not have been an accident. Let us not fall prey to the rumors but instead ask God to guide our actions. Remember, my sisters and brothers, vengeance in your hands only leads to more pain. Vengeance is mine, saith the Lord. In the worst of the worst of times, we must trust God." He sang low, softly, "Amazing Grace."

"Oh my Lord, my baby!" screamed someone from the front pew, and the whole place erupted in wailing moans.

One young woman in the front row was so distraught that she had to be carried out. It was Fay. Two women called her name when she ran to the coffin. They tried to calm her, as she tried to grab the corpse and take it with her. She threw herself over Sean's upper body, completely covering his face, and managed to get her arms underneath the hard, cold, stone-like version of a man.

Reverend Reid tried to calm the flock. The crying and moaning were endless, until in the midst of everything, the saxophonist stopped playing. Reverend Reid stopped singing and stood still, looking at the back of the church, causing just about everyone to shift in their seats and angle their heads to the back of the church.

Breanna stood in the center of the aisle alone, out of place, bewildered. Her makeup was haphazardly applied to her face, more to one side than the other. She walked up the aisle toward the casket in a full-length fur coat, despite this being the middle of May. The hush that colored the room was straight from the *Twilight Zone*. Her complexion was flushed with strawberry blotches covering most of her face.

"Get her out of here!" someone hollered.

"What is she doing here? Get her out!" someone else hollered.

Reverend Reid stood still as his slanted eyes held the sight of Breanna tightly.

Several men surrounded Breanna and escorted her to the back of the church. They escorted her with such force I thought that they were going to beat her up right there in church. Their faces were fixed in anger, their eyes bulging with wide, wild rage.

I jumped up and out of my seat while they shoved her out of the door, practically throwing her down the steps.

"Breanna," I called, trying to catch her as she slumped to the ground. "Why are you here? How? Where is your brother?"

"Sean!" she screamed. Her eyes were wide, red, and fixed on the doors of the church. I could have been anybody; she didn't even recognize me. "Sean," she cried. "I am so sorry, Sean."

The guys were still standing at the doors of the church, looking at us, including the sarcastic uncle who read the obituary. "Get her out of here," the tall one said to me.

"Come on!" I hurried her away from the church as other mourners were starting to emerge with hate-filled glares. "We have to get you out of here." Breanna quieted a little, but felt weightless as I placed her arm around my neck and tried to force her to stay on her feet to get to the car parked a block away. One of her shoes fell off, but I couldn't stop to pick it up. My heart was pounding fast. I rushed ahead to escape the angry pack that followed closely.

"How the hell did you get here, anyway?" I asked. I ran the last few yards to my car, then opened the door to toss her in. She was not fighting me now. Instead she was like a robot, just going along with whatever I said. "Get in, lock the door, and don't move. What are you doing here? Are you crazy?" *That* just might be the case.

A few people rushed toward the car just as I pulled out of my parking spot. A beefy guy even followed me down the block, screaming something I couldn't hear because the windows were closed and Breanna was crying. My heart was pounding loudly.

"Please don't take me home, Spiegel. Puh-leeze, take me back. I want to see Sean. I don't care. Please take me back."

"Breanna!" I yelled. I jerked the car over to the side of the road when we were a safe distance from Sean's friends and family. "You've got to pull yourself together. It was an accident. You've got to pull yourself together. You must go home. What if we have to leave for Bermuda? You've got to get it together. Do you hear me?"

"Spiegel, I am sorry. I have to see Sean. I want to make sure he is all right. Spiegel, please." She looked at me squinting her eyes as though she was trying to remember my face.

"You are not making sense." I shook her. "Sean is dead. Breanna, you know that. You may be on trial for his death. You may be on trial for your very own life. You've got to get a hold of yourself."

"Please don't take me home!" she screamed, "Please don't tell Dad that I was here." Suddenly she gasped. "I can't breathe." She choked in short, panting breaths. "I can't breathe, Spiegel."

"Breathe, Breanna. Bend over. Place your head between your legs, quickly. Come on, Breanna, Breanna."

"Please, Spiegel," she said again, "Please don't take me home."

"I must, Breanna. You should go home and stay there."

Home was the safest place for her, absent a stay in the psycho-ward, so we drove in silence toward it.

"But what about Sean? Where is he going?"

I wasn't sure what to say next, but before I knew it the words flew out of my mouth, "The Mt. Airy Cemetery, Breanna, the cemetery."

She was pale. She sat frozen, mumbling, "The cemetery?"

Chapter Five

Several weeks had passed since Sean's funeral. Breanna had not returned to the island because she was just too ill. In the meantime, Bermuda had waited, but now our time was up. I was scheduled to depart one hot afternoon in June when Craig stopped by my office to wish me happy birthday. "Hey, baby," he said. "You are one hard lady to git wit, know what I'm sayin'?" I laughed at his Ebonics. "Surprise!"

The case had preoccupied my every waking moment. Unfortunately, that didn't leave much time for a personal life. "Hi, Sweetie," I said and got up to close my office door. Craig swirled around to face me and handed me a dozen fully bloomed red roses.

"Marry me, girl!" he teased. He was always teasing me. "Your wish is my command," he said as he kissed me gently. "Happy Birthday."

I walked over to my desk, laid the roses down, and pressed the intercom button to ask my secretary to hold my calls. "Thank you, Craig," I said, wrapping my arms around his neck and brushing his handsome face with the tips of my fingers. "What a nice surprise."

His kisses on my forehead and cheeks felt so comforting. I hugged him as he swooped me up onto my desk and pulled my skirt up to my waist, exposing to his face *our* little secret—I wasn't wearing panties. "Craig?" He smiled and I gasped as his tongue eased up to tease me.

I leaned back on my desk and the scent of roses intoxicated me. Craig burrowed into my wetness. I lost my sense of reason, freely and shamelessly, while Craig delved deeper with every penetration of his magical tongue.

"Happy birthday to me," danced into my mind to the rhythm of Craig's sexy bobbing red head. "Oh yes. That's the spot." Happy birthday to me, I lost *it* as I squeezed his face between my thighs. Craig found *it* and continued stroking me for more. Happy Birthday to me, happy birthday, *dear* me. My office door creaked.

"Craig!" I pushed him back and we both collected ourselves. "Did you hear someone?"

I felt flushed when Walter knocked and then opened my door. "We better get going," Walter said, gesturing for me to follow. He ignored the fact that I had company. I awkwardly kissed Craig good-bye, thanked him for the roses, and fell in step behind Walter. We had a good two hours before the plane left for Bermuda. What was the rush?

Walter was moving swiftly through the parking lot to his brand-spanking new Mercedes 450 sedan. We jumped in and took off. A sweet tobacco aroma filled his car. I prayed that he couldn't smell the scent of Craig, sex, and me that lingered in the air, and that he hadn't peeked before he knocked.

Walter drove fast as he spoke. "Felix is convinced that he can somehow use his influence to make this entire situation go away."

"What do you think?"

Walter shook his head and grabbed his pipe from the ashtray. "This is not going to blow over." Walter stopped at a red light. "We got it on good authority that they don't have enough to arrest her. See what you can find out though."

I listened intently. Although I'd been practicing for ten years, criminal defense was Walter's area of expertise. He was considered a bulldog lawyer. He even looked a little like a bulldog, often blowing up his face with a puckered brow.

Walter did everything fast. He walked fast, talked, and even ate quickly. I smiled at the thought of him even fucking his wife in a rush. He kept talking. "Find out as much as you can about any witnesses in the area on that night." The rhythm and blues of WDAS FM humming on the radio surprised me. I pegged Walter to be a smooth jazz listener.

"Who am I meeting first?" Seventy-nine degrees outside and he had his air on. "Can you turn the air conditioner down or off?"

He hesitated, then laughed. "My wife hates the air too. The local counsel will pick you up from the airport." He pulled into the airport parking lot, turned the car off and jumped out. "The district attorney there is also expecting you." He paused. "Remember, though, that they call their district attorney, director of public prosecution."

When Walter and I entered the airport, I was dismayed to see a crowd of reporters with cameras and microphones clustered there. It was a media circus. Cameras and questions flashed as I tried to collect my thoughts, somewhat unprepared to make a statement so soon.

"Is this a crime of passion?" "Is it true that you quit your job to defend the Congressman's daughter?" "Will she be returning to Bermuda?" "Has she confessed to the murder?"

Walter loved the spotlight. Reporters jostled him and he jostled them back. He put me in the line of fire today though. "Has she confessed to the murder?" was as good a place as any to start.

I fussed with my hair for a quick second, pulling it back in a bun at the nape of my neck with a light blue ribbon matching my blue cotton blouse and khaki skirt. I began, "Breanna Jordan is being sought for questioning in an accident on the island of Bermuda." I tried to remember the do's and don'ts about lawyers talking to the press, the whole pre-trial publicity angle, but wanted to push my way through the crowd and join Walter, who was holding the elevator door. Rule number one—give them something. No comment is a sign of guilt. The tables were already starting to turn in my legal career; it used to be Walter in front of the microphone. Who had leaked that I had been retained to represent Breanna and that I had quit my job?

In the midst of all of the excitement, I looked right into the dark eyes of someone uncomfortably familiar, although I was not at all sure how I knew him. He was very tall, a big guy. He stood with reporters, although he clearly was not a reporter, as he had no visible interest in asking me questions, no pen or pencil no note pad or microphone. Yet he studied me intently and when my eyes met his stare he quickly backed away from the crowd.

"Media frenzy?" I said while waiting to board the plane. "It has been this way from the start. Should we bring in a media consultant?"

"Maybe, not a bad idea," Walter said. The press moved fast and we didn't want them to try and convict Breanna before she'd had her day in court.

On board the plane and settled in my window seat, I pulled out my phone. I had a number of messages from my secretary with the 411 on office gossip. I hadn't seen much of James in the past weeks, but there was a message from him saying he'd missed me. I kept pressing the replay button to hear the anticipation and wanting in his voice.

About two hours later, we landed in Bermuda to a warm eighty-eight degrees and sunny, typical weather for late June. We coasted to a stop and the attendants wheeled a metal staircase up to the door. We walked single file down the flight of steps into the airport.

The cute little airport was bright, airy, and very clean. Not a speck of litter anywhere. A portrait of Her Majesty, the head of state, Queen Elizabeth II, graced the wall. After clearing customs and tracking down my luggage, I saw a gentleman wearing navy blue Bermuda shorts and a matching cap, carrying a white sign with black letters that read, Spiegel Cullen—Philadelphia.

I walked up to him and introduced myself.

"Ms. Cullen, Mr. King has sent me to drive you to your hotel stay." King was the local counsel I was scheduled to meet later that day. "Welcome to Bermuda," he said with a heavy British accent. "I will take you to the hotel and Mr. King will meet you there in an hour."

"Thank you," I said. "How far is the hotel?" My mom had taught me to always ask the distance when taking a taxi in an unfamiliar place to make sure it jives with your understanding.

"You are staying at the Marriott—yes?" He asked me to please follow him to his taxi. A slender man with strong features and small legs, muscular and tight, he looked past retirement age but fit. "First time in Bermuda?" He grinned and continued, "Marriott is very close to airport—maybe ten minutes. It is the hotel you saw from the plane as you were landing—the three-tier castle-like building."

As if on vacation, an instant feeling of calm covered me—the one I usually get when my feet touch down on an island. "Yes, this is my first time in Bermuda." What gave me away? Could it have been the sheer excitement on my face as I looked from side to side as he drove along narrow winding roads on the way to the hotel? "So many flowers."

"Free to grow wild here." Hibiscus and lilies jutting from flourishing green plants and trees, dotted the path as we traveled.

"Are those houses up there in the hills?"

"Yes. I live up there on the right."

"In the hills?" I asked leaning forward.

He laughed and said, "Yes."

I was slightly embarrassed at my assumption that only wealthy people lived in the hills. He smiled, a few missing teeth complemented his reddish brown complexion.

I focused on safer subjects—or at least my eyes did. The sun bouncing off the clearest turquoise waters in the western Atlantic sparkled. Spurts of pink and fuchsia oleander bloomed between hedges of roses, cherry trees, and hibiscus unlike anything I'd ever seen. "It looks like every flower in the world is here."

"Our climate is prime for plant life," he said, and began to give me a history lesson about the world's oldest British colony, Bermuda, discovered in 1503 by an explorer named Juan de Bermudez. Blue skies, no pollution, and no blockbuster movie billboards added to the charm of the day. But, the narrow, sharply twisting roads were a little scary. Arrows along the way marked *Railway Trail* caught my eye.

"What is a Railway Trial?" I asked.

"Dirt tracks cut all through the island for walking and running," he answered. "It used to be our railway system, but Bermuda converted it for tourists many years ago."

Continuing my backseat sightseeing tour, I took a deep breath at those intersections where only a frail wooden rail separated the road from the ocean. I was totally befuddled with the way people drove the cars on the left-hand side of the road, turned right into a far left lane, and how well the islanders had mastered their driving skills on some pretty narrow roads, not to mention those roundabouts. Non-Bermudians were not all allowed to drive on the island. Mopeds, yes. Cars, no. Buses and taxis were the vehicles of choice for tourist.

We arrived at the hotel in ten minutes or so, just as the taxi driver had said. My room, several floors up, had a balcony that overlooked open terrain of grass and the bluest water. No commercial skyscrapers obstructing the panoramic view of the island or polluting the air, according to Felix.

By the time I had showered and taken a quick nap, the local legal team called from the lobby. I took the elevator to meet them. In the lobby, two men were comfortably conversing and laughing. "Hello," I said. "I think that you are expecting me, Spiegel Cullen."

They both looked puzzled. One, the one wearing a deep tan, informed me that the two were waiting for their wives.

"I'm sorry," I said and moved further into the lobby.

"You must be Spiegel Cullen."

"Yes, hello."

"Dirk Smith." He extended his hand. A warm, confident man wrapped tightly in a six-foot-four frame, Dirk had nice long legs, slightly bowed. I extended my hand to meet his firm grip. The fine Bermudian brother's muscular body expanded well beyond his clothes. He was coffee-brown, sporting a bald head and an incredible pair of dimples. He was sensual just standing still.

"Dirk?" I confirmed.

"Yes." His smile lit up his face. Nice straight white teeth. "Please join us over here," he said in an easy island accent, and stepped back to extend his arm to let me walk past him in the direction of the other gentleman, who was now standing and waiting for us.

"Hello, Spiegel Cullen, I am Stephen King," he said. "Welcome to Bermuda, albeit under less than ideal circumstances."

"Stephen, yes, hello." I paused. " Stephen King—what a name."

"Yes, I'm taking time out to defend clients from real horror— prison life," he said with a heavy dose of sarcasm and a light British accent.

Walter had told me that Stephen was sensitive about his name. He'd even considered changing it once or twice, but thought better of it because he was actually Stephen King the fourth and, believe it or not, his son was Stephen King the fifth. Stephen was almost the equal opposite of Dirk on first glance. A man of small stature, his complexion was fair and his smile quick, though hidden considerably behind his goatee.

Both Stephen and I followed Dirk to the hotel's restaurant. We exchanged casual talk while waiting to be seated.

We sat at a square table near a window overlooking the curving manicured grounds of the hotel. Done with my fish and chips faster than either Stephen or Dirk, I wiped my hands and readied to pull out a yellow pad and pen. They both had at least another piece of fish and a few more fries to consume. I pulled my tablet out anyway.

The mood was stiff and professional when Dirk said, in his nice British tone of voice, "I have photos of the crime scene." He stopped and began again, "On the day we found the body, we thought drowning. But, a brother and his girl claim to have been sleeping in the back of their car and woke up in time to see a young lady."

Stephen, who had been quiet, now said, "I have a copy of their statement back at the office. But, the only thing they saw was a girl rushing off on a moped."

Dirk reached into his shirt pocket and handed me a piece of paper. "Here is a sketch of the person they said they saw leaving the scene. Does it resemble your client in any way?"

"Who drew this?" I said with unexpected anger, which I thought answered his question and Dirk's waiting stare.

"Dirk was one of the first investigators on the scene," Stephen said and gave Dirk a friendly elbow. "We worked together on the force before I went to law school. Good guy, he is." He patted Dirk on the back.

Dirk blushed slightly but kept the mood professional. "We can take you to where the body was found," Dirk said. He brushed his tongue across his plump upper lip. "It was on the south end of the island."

We piled into Stephen's small car and drove off to the spot.

※ ※ ※ ※

As we approached Horseshoe Beach, my heart sank. The sharp bend opening to the beach was narrow with boulders on the left and the right. Mostly mopeds were parked in a small area for cars. A few feet from the mopeds, a steep cliff overlooked a collection of sand dunes, big boulders, and jutting rock formations extending to the water.

Stephen pointed to the top of one of the sharp edged cliffs and said, "We think that that is where he fell." Then, he asked, "Would you like to trot up to the spot?"

I nodded, heart racing.

"Did you know that his family came here to claim the body?" I shook my head no and he finished, "They were pretty mad, calling your client the 'black spider.' They don't think that it was an accident, and they voiced their opinions to the press and to anyone who would listen. Apparently, Sean was a loved gent. There were at least fifty people here trying to find out what happened."

We stood on the beach. The sand was a mixture of cream and pink. Little yellow-belly birds played along the white fuzz from the gush of the waves surging endlessly from the crystal blue waters onto the powdery sand. Brown-skinned girls in neon-colored thong bikinis looked twice at Dirk as we walked by. "I knew right away Sean was from the States," Dirk said. "The dude had on silk pants and one red alligator shoe. His body washed ashore over there." Dirk held out his muscular arm.

We took off our shoes and socks and left them on the beach then walked toward the jutting rocks. I followed closely behind Stephen, and we traveled down a steep rocky embankment to where the body washed ashore. He extended his hand to help me along the rough steps. When we got to the spot, I just stood there for a few moments to collect my thoughts.

Stephen pointed toward even rockier terrain. "It appears he drifted out to sea for a day or so and later washed up."

The bottoms of our pants were soaked.

Stephen said, "Be careful."

A serious chill ran through my veins, even though the warmth of the water swirled around my feet.

Dirk swept his tongue across his upper lip again. "At first we assumed the poor guy had come too close and fell. But, the way his head was banged up matched the profile of an open investigation here of two other bodies that washed ashore. For a day it was being reported as another seashore killing until other things didn't match up."

"Like what?"

"In *Seashore*, the men had been killed someplace else and then dumped in the water." Dirk was so cool. He seemed to be the kind of guy that remained calm under any circumstances.

"The men were dead when they hit the water, I take it?"

"Exactly. Your guy," he said in jest, "definitely drowned."

"They say his lungs contained both water and air," Stephen interjected.

"He was pretty beat up," Dirk said.

"Really?" I queried.

"He could have hit the rocks when he fell," Stephen said.

My head was spinning with thoughts of how to get Breanna out of this mess. "What about the witnesses?" I asked. "Have they said anything consistent with a fall?"

"Nope," Stephen said.

A man's voice called from behind, "Hey, Steve." I had seen the short, stocky, bearded guy earlier and had thought he was a tourist because of the camera. He was a reporter. "Got anything for us?"

"Nothing," Stephen shouted back. The guy kept his distance but stood and watched us as we walked back down a path to the beach.

Dirk said, "We had divers in the water all day, searching for clues—perhaps another body, a boat, something, anything. The dude had all of his clothes on, but his pants were twisted around his ankles. Wallet was in his back left pocket. We called his family right away and his brother told us that he was here with a girl."

I stared out at the rippling blue water. Three sailboats glided across the waters in a single line.

Dirk continued, "It was eerie. I peered down at the frozen gaze of the man, and wondered what had brought him to this end, so prematurely." His voice echoed with concern. "The guy was the same age as me, thirty-two." He shook his head.

Stephen added, "Was it an accident? Was it a drug deal gone bad? We never suspected a woman until the witnesses said they heard the rustling of a moped and saw a pretty lady rush off like she was being chased by a red devil."

"She is very beautiful." Dirk paused. "The drawing was done by a police artist. It was being circulated on the island." The laughter of kids playing on paddleboats in the water caught our attention. "Are you ready to go?"

"Okay. I should call Walter as well."

"When are you meeting with our director of public prosecution?" Dirk asked.

"Tomorrow."

"The last word I got," Stephen said, "is that they are sending extradition papers along with an indictment to the Bermuda Ministry of Foreign Affairs." He tucked both hands in and out of his pockets. "They want the American girl."

We inched along the beach to gather our shoes, kicking the hot sand from our shoes and socks to little avail. We drove back to my hotel room, barely uttering a word.

We left our sand-filled shoes at the door and sat at the small round table in my room.

"It was an accident, right?" Dirk asked.

"Right," I said. "Stephen, is there an extradition treaty between Bermuda and the United States?"

"It is probably a situation of goodwill between the states," he said. "I suppose, given the status of the congressman. If he's in with the right people, this matter will be dealt with speedily." He smirked. "But the crime was committed here in our jurisdiction, therefore if there is a trial, it will be here on our soil."

"What do I have to do to practice here?"

Stephen replied, "We can work that out. You'd need a work permit. The process takes about a year before you are called to practice, as we call it." He paused.

"Any way we could speed up the process?"

"A year, give or take." Stephen pulled papers from a folder and handed them to me. "What about Walter?"

"Walter's already admitted." I said.

Stephen laughed as he and Dirk prepared to leave my room. Once they left, I called Walter. "They want the American girl," echoed in my ear.

"Walter, it's Spiegel."

"Hey."

"Are you ready for the bad news?"

"What?"

"There was a couple in a car, making out or something, who may be possible witnesses. They gave the police a sketch—"

"A what? Of what?" Walter's voice elevated.

"Of a girl they saw leaving the crime scene."

"What did they see, exactly?"

"I'll find out more tomorrow, right now all I know is that they saw someone that resembled Breanna leave the scene in a hurry."

"Witnesses? Kiss my dick!"

"Yes," I said. "What are your thoughts so far on defense? Have you any more thoughts to what we discussed concerning the motion for change of venue?"

"There's no real evidence that a trial held in Bermuda would not be fair, and we don't want to anger the courts, especially if we lose the fucking motion."

"Have someone pull the research anyway on the change of venue issue." I vowed to leave no stone unturned.

"It supports what I just said. Let's look at possible defenses."

"Accident? Self defense? Insanity?" I paused. "PMS?"

"What?"

"I've done some research on a pre-menstrual stress syndrome defense."

"A what?"

"In extreme cases—"

"How about fucking spoiled goddamn brat? She's smart enough to know better," he yelled. "Kiss my dick!"

"Would you stop saying *that?*"

"What are you saying? Please tell me something."

"Look, if they charge her with murder, she's doomed unless we come up with extenuating circumstances."

"I don't know if PMS would fit into that category though," he said. "You mentioned it before and I didn't like it then and I don't like it now."

"I think it does. You said yourself that psychological disposition can be an extenuating circumstance."

"I am *not* going into court on any PMS voodoo. Has she even been diagnosed with this? Do you even *get* diagnosed with it?"

I had read cases, but they did not come to mind fast enough so I said, "I know they joke about PMS, but for some people it can be a real problem. Give me a little rope to talk with a doctor."

"Rope to choke!" he countered. "I don't like it. The guy may have tripped over his own fucking feet."

"Perhaps."

Walter continued to rant and rave. "PMS?" I could still hear him even after we said good-bye and I lowered the receiver from my ear to hang up the phone. "What the hell is that? I don't like it!"

I certainly understood Walter's apprehension about my raising such a questionable defense. Any suggestion that we're trying to wiggle out of a tried-and-proven avenue for the defense would result in negative press and worse, especially if we were to lose. Even so, I couldn't let it rest because I wasn't so sure that it was an accident. How would I ever convince a jury?

Chapter Six

I wrestled with sleep last night. Not knowing what to expect from Bermuda's district attorney troubled me, along with a sudden uneasy feeling of being watched. I packed my stuff and switched hotels. The Elbow Beach Hotel was only a few miles from where Breanna had stayed with Sean.

No one knew I switched hotels, so the ringing phone jolted me upright.

"Good morning, love," came the voice on the other end.

Who had found me so soon?

"Good morning, love."

Silence.

I still didn't recognize the voice.

"Craig?" I asked.

"Craig? Who the hell is Craig?" It was James who asked.

"None'ya."

"I thought we were beyond the 'none'ya' stage," James said.

Actually, I was glad he'd called. "I didn't catch your voice at first."

"You were expecting someone else?" he teased.

"Obviously!" I teased him back. "What's up?" I smiled.

"I have a flight into Bermuda today at eleven. Will you meet me at the airport?"

He was coming to Bermuda? "I have a meeting with the district attorney this morning," I said. "Why are you coming today?"

"Dad wants me there—a show of good faith, I guess. The news hounds are busy. Even *Court TV* called the house the other day."

"What did you tell them?"

He chucked as he said, "I told them to speak to Walter."

"Good. Did you give them the number?"

"No. I hung up the phone." He stopped chuckling long enough to say, "Let them get the number from the phone book."

He could be such a smart-ass. "Give them my number if they contact you again. There is too much at stake."

"*Right*. Breanna is walking around like some crazy girl with an attitude." James took a quick breath. "And, to top things off, my father will do *whatever it takes* to protect her, even to the point of jeopardizing his position. He has always jumped through hoops for her."

"What are you talking about?" I tossed the covers and stood up to stretch. I walked over to the window and opened the drapes to the view. The water was calm, the day clear. Private sailboats floated in the waters off the docks of pastel colored houses.

"Maybe now," James continued, "Breanna will grow up and stop looking for my father to get her out of shit." He paused. "Congress is about to recess for the summer anyway."

"You sound a little jealous." Odd—I'd never heard James talk like this about his sister before.

"I have something I want to talk with *you* about."

"Go."

"Not like this. I want to see you, talk with you in person."

"What's up, James? Scheduling conversation is not an option."

"I'll see you when I get there." He slammed the telephone in my ear.

The heavy sloshing of the waves filled the room as I opened the window, and felt the urge to jog along the beach.

I inhaled the crisp smog-free air of Bermuda's dawn. At barely six-thirty, the chatter of room service knocking on doors and clanging china and trays of breakfast treats competed with the stillness of the morning. I put on my running gear, laced up a new pair of sneakers, and placed a quick call to Craig. I smiled.

He answered the telephone on the first ring. "Hello." His voice was deep, as though he'd been partying all night.

I missed him more when I heard his voice. "I was thinking about you."

"What time will you get in?" he asked.

"It won't be for a few more days."

"Oh."

"I'm meeting with their district attorney to see how they will charge her."

"Will she have to return to Bermuda?"

"Eventually, yes."

"Yeah. I heard the authorities are not so sure that it was an accident."

"What else have you heard?"

"Nothing. One of the girls, scratch that, one of the reporters at the station is headed to Bermuda."

"Have I met her?" I had met most of the men reporters at Craig's station but not many of the female reporters.

"I don't think you've met her." Craig cleared his throat. "How are you doing, baby?"

I hesitated, but then said, "I wish that you were here with me."

"I can be there," he quickly offered.

"I'm too busy for fun, though, Craig. I probably won't even get a chance to see much of the island."

Someone knocked on the door.

Craig heard it too and asked edgily, "*Who* is that knocking on *your* door so early in the morning?"

"It's my breakfast, silly." I went to the door to let the server in with my toast and orange juice.

"I may be coming that way anyway, with a friend from high school."

"What?"

"An old friend. She recently went through a messy divorce and wants to hang out on a beach."

Excuse me—did he just say *she*? "What?" Annoyance creeped into my voice. I picked up a piece of toast and then tossed it back on the plate. I'd lost my appetite.

"She is just an old friend, Spiegel, nothing remotely romantic. She called to tell me about her divorce. She mentioned wanting to retreat to an island. I knew that you were in Bermuda, so I suggested . . ."

"Craig, let me talk to you a little later. Am I supposed to understand?" He was crazy. I often live in my head, thinking more than I actually say. I couldn't understand in that instant why I was letting him silence me. Tell him he'd lost his mind!

"*Spiegel*, don't let your mind go wandering. Yolanda is *just* a friend."

"*Yeah*." I didn't say anything else. Silenced.

"Do you want to talk about this later?" he asked.

"No. Good-bye," I finally said.

"Bye?" he said and I felt my insides turn upside down.

Dating be damned, I thought, but reminded myself that Craig was a good catch. I opted to let it go for the moment and call him that evening to find out more about this *friend*.

I left messages for Stephen, Walter, and my secretary, giving them my new location, and headed out the door for a morning run. In the hallways, the scents of bacon and hot buttered biscuits flavored the air. I leaned against the wall of the hotel for a moment to stretch my legs.

The tall slender doorman greeted me with a warm smile. "Good day," he said eyeing my backside.

Waving, I took off on what would probably be a long run. I was going to run until I figured out what I was doing with James, Craig, Breanna, and the district attorney—there was lots of stuff to think about.

A tad bit chilly for summer was the first thing I felt when I reached the beach. The beach was clear straight ahead for miles except for the seagulls pecking at the cracked crabs and washed up jellyfish. A good ten minutes into the jog, I could feel my temperature rising. Tranquility filled me as I took in the moist breath of the blue sea and felt the warmth of the air hitting my face. Miles of hilly terrain off in the distance comforted me until I got the eeriest feeling that a guy jogging behind me was following me. I glanced over my shoulders and the guy slowed to a walk. He was tall, a big guy from what I could tell. I decided to run a little faster, but the wet sand underfoot slowed me down. I emerged into a grassy clearing that was slowly being reclaimed by the sea, surrounded by naturally sculptured boulders pushing up from the earth. No one else close by, the stranger was gaining on me. I saw his face now. A stab of apprehension filled me as I tried not to meet his rude gaze. He was a black guy, nice looking, not likely to do me any harm, not in the midst of such raw beauty. Not here. Not now. I continued running along the beach. I was sweating more from fear than running. I didn't want to turn, to do so would acknowledge my fear. I would not stop. He'd catch up to me any second and we'd say, "Hello."

I nearly peed in my shorts when a couple jetted out from a residential path onto the beach. "Hiya! How's it going?" I said. I didn't know why they smiled so warmly but I knew why I smiled. I was safe. The guy had disappeared. Peace had been restored.

I shook off the feeling and darted toward the sign pointing to the Railway Trail. The trail ran along the pink, sandy beach for a short time before turning into a concrete road that fast became a mixture of overturned soil and rubble, steep and rough in some spots. Deep pink oleanders shot out from the bushels of green shrubs. Tall palm and thick pineapple trees provided the backdrop for the island farmers in their straw-hats as they tended to rolling fields of melon crops. The fragrances of pineapple and fresh flowers whipped through the breeze. With the sun pounding at my back as sweat covered me, I paused for a moment to touch the jagged rocks and felt again that I was not alone—but there was no one in sight. Silly me.

By the time I got back to the hotel, Dirk was waiting in the lobby. "Dirk?" I said. "How did you know where to find me?"

"Good morning. I thought I'd give you a ride to the city." He walked closer. "I tried to call this morning, but your line was busy. Stephen told me how to reach you."

"Give me a moment to quick change." I felt like I'd put in a day's work already.

"Fancy yourself a runner, do you?"

"Yes."

"I run also. Bermuda has some great trails. I can show you, if you like."

"Yes, of course," I shouted back at Dirk while bolting toward an open elevator door.

When I returned to the lobby, Dirk stood waiting at the front door to rush me to the director's office, six miles away in the capitol city of Hamilton. Hamilton was the hub of seven main islands of Bermuda and many smaller islands and islets sprinkled in the Atlantic Ocean connected by bridges and ferries. Most tourists, according to my handsome escort, confined themselves to one of the big islands. "I'd like to show you around the island, if you like," Dirk said.

"I'd like that."

"We can start this evening. There is an arts festival at King's Court. Many of the locals will be selling perfumes and goods. I'd like to introduce you to my girls at True Reflections but let me check on the jazz festival also." He paused and flexed a broad smile. "Natalie Cole, Pieces of a Dream, Kenny G will all be there at the jazz fess and you'll have a good time and get some souvenirs for your husband, pretty lady."

"Please do not call me pretty lady," I said. Since becoming a lawyer, I'd become very uncomfortable with the patronizing manner of most of the men in this profession. "And there is no husband." Why did I snap at him?

"It will not happen again." He gave me a half smile, half frown.

I light-heartedly smiled, but wanted to apologize or give some lame excuse for being cranky. "What is True Reflections?"

"A popular little tourist spot." He paused. "Lots of stuff like books, Black greeting cards, calendars, island treasures, T-shirts, you know stuff like that." Dirk made a sharp turn onto a curvy road. "We are here," he announced as we pulled in front of a four-story office building. Barristers bustled importantly about the office. As they walked, they flung greetings over their shoulders to the girl who sat at the desk marked "Information." The girl's complexion was a beautiful bronze. Boy, what most women wouldn't pay to maintain such a beautiful hue.

All of the windows in the office behind her desk were open and from the outside came the banging of car doors and the chatter of a crowd in the courtyard. "Reporters are here," said Dirk, peering out of the window. The slightly wistful eyes of the young woman glanced once at me suspiciously. She wasn't friendly.

"Reporters?" I asked.

The buzzer at the girl's desk sounded, and both Dirk and I looked in her direction. Her agile fingers clicked keys into place. She spoke into the transmitter, "Yes, Mr. Perry." Her fingers tapped a key on her telephone. As she raised her eyes and spoke to Dirk, her voice showed relief. "The director will see you now." She pointed, "Right through those swinging doors, and straight down the corridor to the double doors at the end."

Dirk smiled his thanks, and motioned for me to follow. We walked down a corridor through an open door for the director of public prosecution. A secretary, also with a nice complexion, sat very rigidly behind a desk and nodded toward yet another door marked "Private." I hoped to God that the sun that had kissed these young women would kiss me also, before my time was done. She said, "Right through that door, please."

Kevin Perry, badly in need of a shave, sat in a massive leather swivel chair signing correspondence. He glanced up and said, "Good morning Dirk, and Ms. Cullen, I presume. Take a seat, please." His gaze was back on the letters before he had finished speaking. His pen scrawled a signature when the sun-kissed secretary came in and retrieved a stack of papers. Of slender build, Perry sat hunched at his desk. His hairline was receding, despite his youthful face.

His thin lips parted with the readiness of a Philadelphia politician. "Welcome to Bermuda, most unfortunate of circumstances," he said. "Are you called to practice in Bermuda?"

"Not yet."

"See section 51.52 of the Bermuda Supreme Court Code."

"Yes. We are working on it. Thank you."

Dirk sat quietly in the chair next to me. His dark eyes were watchful and cordial.

"The American girl is your client?" said Perry. He was not so cordial.

"I am here on behalf of my client, Breanna Jordan, and to extend our good faith intention on behalf of her father, Congressman Felix Jordan."

"Yes, I have spoken to Mr. Jordan. I am afraid that we cannot do what he asks of us."

A request had been made? "The United States has pledged its full cooperation," I said.

"As a father, he wants nothing more than for this matter to disappear for him and his family." He stood for the first time and shook my hand. "However, a crime has been committed. We want a fair resolution."

I didn't like being caught off guard. "Fair?" I asked, feeling ill prepared to talk about any special requests.

"Our lady justice is blind. You see, you should expect no special considerations." Perry sat up in his chair. "We have eyewitnesses who placed his daughter at the crime scene. It is believed that the two argued and a fight ensued in which Sean Thomas was killed. We think your client can help us fill in the gaps."

I took a deep breath. "What are you proposing?" The vibes, as they say, were not good and I was not getting the sense that he was willing to "work with us," as Felix had hoped.

"No tricks, Ms. Cullen. No political ploys. Your client must come to Bermuda. Every courtesy will be allowed to you, but . . . there *will be* justice. You must return her to Bermuda."

I stepped lightly. I didn't want to piss him off at our first meting. "I can assure you, Mr. Perry, that we have no intention of political tricks or ploys."

"I know a little of your reputation, Ms. Cullen."

"Excuse me?" What the heck was he talking about?

"The reputation of lawyers in the States—the rush-to-judgment rhetoric in the Simpson case; the what do you call it, the Twinkie defense when the kids killed their parents." He moved to his desk, pulled out a manila folder, and slowly read from one of its sheets. "You are highly respected among your peers; up until now you've prosecuted people who killed. Why have you changed your stripes?"

I stood and placed both hands outstretched on his desk. "Mr. Perry, I am not on trial." Already the air between us had turned bad. Dirk sat and watched. "I should let you know that my client is currently under psychiatric evaluation."

"Oh," he said, with a raised brow. "If you think that you are going to assert some sort of insanity defense . . . not here in Bermuda, Ms. Cullen."

"Are you seeking to charge my client?"

He did not answer right away. Instead he offered, "Citizens of the island, and the world for that matter, must be able to live here in peace and enjoy the calm of our island."

I asked again, "Are you seeking to charge my client?"

"If necessary, we will file extradition papers if your client is not in my office in forty-eight hours."

"Can't this wait until after the holiday?" I'd planned to be home for the Fourth of July.

"Forty-eight hours."

"On what grounds?"

"Suspicion of murder."

"What about the *Seashore* killer? Are you even considering that Sean's death—"

"We don't think the two incidents are related!"

Perry tossed an envelope in front of me and circled his long narrow index finger for me to open it. I did.

"She panicked," I said looking at seven or eight photographs of the corpse of Sean Thomas.

Dirk got up from his seat and stood next to me as I flipped through the photos. Other than the crumbled pants around his ankles, Sean was dressed. Bloodstains on the left side of his loosely buttoned shirt were huge. The photos were gruesome.

"She panicked," I repeated, trying not to throw up.

"Is that what they call murder in your country?"

I did not answer. Instead, I looked from the photos and stared for a moment into the flat eyes of the prosecutor. His eyes were still and cold. His posture was stiff, like the body of a dead street cat.

Chapter Seven

Yesterday's meeting with the prosecutor was rough. We were in for a fight. I'd overslept and woke to a loud ringing phone.

"I got the job!"

"Aliá?" I sat straight up in bed and focused on the morning light peering in the window.

"Yes, wake up." Aliá's voice was full of excitement on the other end of the telephone.

"I'm up. Congratulations. What job?" I had been up all night reading through the case law on pre-menstrual stress syndrome that Walter had faxed me, with the word *risky* underscored.

"Your sister is now the fashion editor for *Esteem*. Spi, you hear me? I got the job!" She screeched. "Me. Jessica Aliá Cullen." Aliá's name suits her so well we never call her Jessica. She's an Aliá.

"I am proud of you, Sis! When I get back, we'll celebrate." Wow. *Esteem* puts out this great ritzy magazine, *Pep*. I bet they got thousands of applications.

"When are you coming home?" she sighed dramatically. "You've been there for over a week."

"Another week or so."

"I still can't believe Brea is in the middle of this craziness," Aliá said. "Yeah. I saw her yesterday. We went to the MAC store at the mall."

She's out shopping for makeup? "How is she?"

"Better, but she is scared shitless. Her father screens all of her calls. She can't go anywhere alone."

"He's just trying to protect her."

"I think they're leaving for Bermuda today. Right?"

"Yeah, the arraignment is tomorrow."

"What exactly is that?" Aliá asked.

"Where they read the charges against her and she can plead not guilty."

"Maybe I should come to Bermuda. We can spend July 4th in Bermuda! How about that?"

"What about your job?" I asked.

"Fashion editor!" she screamed. "I am so excited. But, I don't start until July 10th."

I looked around the room for the digital clock. "I'll call you later, Ms. Editor."

"Hey, what's going on with Craig?"

"He arrives today. He's visiting with a *friend.*"

"What do you mean, 'visiting with a friend'?" This would not be one of those quick two or three-minute conversations that we typically have throughout the day.

"I know, a girl." Aliá didn't like Craig, so I should have kept *that* detail to myself.

"Love you, Sis. Say the word and I'll be on the plane to Bermuda. I can just kick Craig's ass."

"Aliá, Craig is at least three times your size." Aliá, who is petite, but incredibly shapely, had worked out two days in her entire twenty-six years of life, but was built like an hourglass. Oh, forgive me; she does love to dance.

"*I'll tell you what,* I can beat him! How is he going to bring someone to Bermuda when you are there? That shit is not right."

"I'm not worried about other women," I told her, trying more to reassure myself.

"Why?" I could picture Aliá with one hand on her hip, and the other holding the telephone tightly. "Why? You don't have a ring on your finger."

"I'm not trying to get married." I paused. "There is nothing that I want to do that I don't do," I said trying to convince someone who knew me better.

"I know you want a family."

"Yeah. The bio clock is ticking and I'd like to have a kid before I—"

"Go to the sperm bank!" she yelled, laughing in the phone. "Go get the sperm if all you want is the kid."

"Girl, you are nuts."

"Who doesn't want the big dream, the rock and the wedding?"

"Me. I don't need it." Denial confirmed.

We laughed the habitual laugh that came at the end of the sentence when we're not sure of the next.

"Did you tell Mom and Dad the good news about the job?"

"Not yet. You were the first one I called." She hesitated. "Have you met anything nice-looking?"

"I met a nice detective on our case. I'd like for you to meet him."

"What are you going to do today?"

"Did you feed my babies?"

"I was at your place yesterday. Yes, I watered your plants. You had two calls from a Dr. Tyler and about seventeen hang-up calls." Dr. Michael Tyler was the psychologist who had been meeting with Breanna for the past few weeks, and his preliminary report was one of the things I was anxious to read. "Is all okay though?" she continued.

If I told Aliá that I thought someone was stalking me, she'd be on the plane immediately. "Absolutely," I said. "It's impossible to feel any other way on this island. It is so pretty."

"Mommy says you push yourself too hard." She paused. "Did you even bring a bathing suit?"

"Uh-huh, uh-huh," I said. "This telephone call is going to cost you a fortune."

"Yeah. I figure I may need to borrow a few dollars from you anyway, to get my wardrobe together for my new job." She chuckled.

"Bye, Aliá."

I walked over to draw the curtains. A balmy day for late June confirmed my plans to spend most of the day inside reading Tyler's report.

We had arranged for Breanna's arrest and release, and she was scheduled to arrive tomorrow. Stephen was handling the preliminary hearing and arraignment where they would officially read the charges.

I had a great view of Bermuda from my window. Homes like villas, the kind you see along the waters in Italy, sat on the opposite side of my hotel suite separated by a vast open channel of sea. Ferries bobbed along in the water. The chugging of their engines filled the air. You couldn't go too many places in Bermuda where you weren't surrounded by the sea. Stephen called and invited me to dinner with his wife and two small tots. I wanted to see how far I'd get with the paperwork before I stopped, so I said perhaps I'd come later.

Instead of getting up, I dozed off until almost three, then ordered buffalo wings, cheese fries, and a Coke. If I'd substitute the Coke with a Mountain Dew I'd have Aliá's favorite meal. I devoured it and turned my attention to Dr. Tyler's report.

Re: Jordan, Breanna
     MRN04002266

"The patient, who is twenty-five years old, with known stress and bouts of pre-menstrual stress syndrome, said her symptoms were aggravated by an incident involving the death of her thirty-one year-old boyfriend. She states she has trouble concentrating and sleeping since the incident that occurred on the island of Bermuda. She reports no history of mental illness or other health concerns. Her family history is negative of mental illness. Her mother died eleven years ago of breast cancer. She has tested HIV negative in the past. Although she is single, patient says she is monogamous, and she says her recent partner was engaged to someone other that the patient, but has never fathered children. She reports no history of STD."

"On general observation, the patient appears to be suffering from stress, trauma, and anxiety. She reports periodic use of Atavin for anxiety. Although there is no concrete evidence of mental illness, on several occasions she has appeared flirtatious in a manner uncharacteristic of her normal demeanor. For example, on several occasions in my office she unbuttoned her blouse to waist level, attempting to undress for a physical examination. She was told repeatedly that this would not be necessary, but she continued to undress until she was nude. My nurse was called into the room and she (the patient) dressed and became very accommodating with the presence of the third person."

"I would recommend daily therapy and medication until emotional balance is completely restored. Further, it is recommended that she undergo a complete health physical, including hormone testing, to determine what effects, if any, the reported bouts of pre-menstrual stress syndrome have on her mental and emotional states."

I needed a drink. If it weren't my case, I wouldn't have believed this mess. I grabbed the report, changed from my pajamas, and made my way to the bar.

The lobby of the hotel bustled. Guests were arriving and departing, and others were just mingling in the cozy areas set up like a giant living room. I spotted the arrow pointing to the Seashore Grill, a popular bar and restaurant, and went inside. I was startled, shocked really, to see Dirk and Felix sitting at the bar.

I walked over to them and said, "What are you two doing here?" I hadn't expected Felix until later. *Was James around?*

Felix stood for a quick hug. His eyes were bulging out of his head. "Dirk was just telling me that a cabby on the island saw someone other than Breanna with Sean on the beach the night he died."

"Excuse me." I turned to Dirk. "How reliable is your source?"

"A reliable source indeed. His name is King Rooster. He's been hustling cabs for almost forty-years." He wiped his strong chin with the back of his hand. "If he says he saw two people from the States fighting, believe it to be true."

"How did he know that they were from the States?"

Dirk smiled. "We know."

"Felix," I asked, "how is it that the two of you are here?"

Dirk answered, "I picked the congressman and his daughter up from the airport."

"Where is Breanna?" I asked. The manipulator, I thought, thinking of Tyler's report.

Felix motioned for another glass of brandy. "She just went up to the room to change."

"Dirk," I asked, "did your friend say it was a woman?"

"Oh yeah, a woman." He stroked the side of his face. "He said they were having a lover's quarrel." He finished a corner of his glass and licked his lip.

I smiled. "What was he doing there?"

"He was on his way home and thought it strange to see people at that spot." Dirk paused and looked around the room like he was looking for someone. "It's a tricky spot to get to if you don't know where you are going."

"He was on the beach?"

"Yeah. He said the beach. I figure you can talk with him further."

"What was he doing there again?"

Felix sat and listened as Dirk continued. "He actually stopped to uh, relieve himself."

"So he stopped his car and got out?"

"He said that he went over to the beach close enough to see that the couple were no longer arguing. He said he jumped back into his car and *eventually* drove off, but that the two never even noticed him."

"I'd like to speak with him. Can you arrange it soon?"

Dirk's bushy eyebrows rose. "Should I try to track him down now?"

"Yes, absolutely."

Dirk smiled. "I understand," he said. "I just found out about this on the way to the airport to get Felix and his daughter."

"Spiegel," Felix said as he stood up waving his hands for emphasis. "Don't you see? Someone else was there and killed Sean?" He threw up his arms.

"I'll go get the guy tonight so that you can speak with him," Dirk said.

"Did the cabby say what the two people looked like?" I asked recalling that someone had already seen someone resembling Breanna at the cliff that night.

Dirk nodded and turned his attention to Breanna who was headed toward us. "Breanna is a little nervous about tomorrow. I offered dinner," Dirk said. "Would you like to order, Spiegel?"

"I *am* nervous about tomorrow," Breanna confirmed as she joined us at the bar. "But I think if we can find the person who was on the beach with Sean, they may let me go tomorrow." She leaned forward to kiss me.

I bet you're nervous, I thought, but asked her instead, "You know about this?"

"Yes. Dirk mentioned it at the airport." Breanna looked good, considering the last time I saw her. She was wearing a long, elegant red dress with a deep-cut neckline. It followed her form tightly. Her closely cropped hair accentuated the beauty of her oval face and nicely arched brows. Her make-up was flawless, even down to the candy-apple bright red lipstick.

"Are we going to have dinner?" Dirk asked. He stared at Breanna like she was his favorite tootsie pop. She had such a way with men.

"Actually," I interrupted, "the sooner we find out if anyone else was on the beach that night, the better our chances of finding out what really happened to Sean."

"You see," Breanna said, eyes lighting with hope. "I didn't kill Sean. I hit him with the bike, but he was alive when I left. I just know it."

"We will get to the bottom of this," Dirk said. She had Dirk hooked. Just that quick, she had Dirk believing her. *Damn dazzle in distress.*

She looked liked she was playing a part in a play. "I didn't know what I was doing. I was mad."

My attitude came out in my words. "If you can get mad to the point of tossing someone off a cliff, you may need—"

"It was just that in that instant, I lost it."

"We know."

"So, you think I killed him, don't you?" She swayed her neck. "Do you?"

No answer.

The conversation at the dinner table was solemn. Dirk asked the waiter to wrap up what was left of his order of steak and potatoes to go.

"Excuse me, Spiegel. I'd like to walk Dirk out to the car," Felix said once the waiter had delivered Dirk's doggie bag. Dirk got up, shook out his pants, and stood for a second, looking at Breanna. Then he and Felix walked away. Felix took an envelope from his pocket and placed it into Dirk's hand.

"I'd like to walk Dirk to the car myself," Breanna whispered to me, smiling, looking off at her father and Dirk as they moved toward the exit, as if she had forgotten our heated exchange. "I like 'em chocolate like dat."

"Oh?" I said with a smirk. "You look good. Are you feeling okay?" I was trying to regain a professional edge. I was wrong to doubt her.

"I feel better." Breanna turned to face me. "My dad said that everything was going to work out." She wiggled her chair closer to the table. "I'm not too worried."

"What's going on?" I asked.

"Nothing really." Breanna giggled. "Dirk and I have a few things in common." She grinned. "That lip-tongue thing he does." She playfully grabbed my arm and laughed. "Do you think it is a nervous gesture? Every time his tongue brushed his lip, my vagina vibrated."

"Woo."

"He's nice, Spiegel, that's all." Breanna certainly did not look like someone about to be arrested for murder. She simply glowed.

I hated to burst her bubble, but on a more serious note, I said, "Breanna, I read the report from Dr. Tyler."

"Good 'ole Dr. Tyler," Breanna spat. "What did the good 'ole Dr. Tyler have to say?"

"Were you flirting with him?"

"Hardly! He is too serious, Spiegel." Breanna was born a flirt. Her curves and those *double-Ds* stirred attention everywhere she turned. She knew how to work her charm.

She was lying. "Be straight with me, Breanna."

"I am." She hesitated. "Have you met him yet?" She rolled her big greenish eyes. "He may have misunderstood something. Did he say that I was flirting with him?"

I glared at her. "This is no time to be fucking around, Breanna."

"I know, Spiegel, but a girl gets lonely and I'm not trying to put my stuff on a shelf." She laughed. Under different circumstances, I would have laughed with her, but not now. "Anyway," she stopped with the giggles and asked, "Whatever he said is confidential—isn't it?"

"I don't want to take any chances of something like that getting to the other side. It makes you out to look manipulative or crazy, you decide."

"But isn't it confidential?"

"If they file a motion for your medical records, they could get them."

"You won't let that happen?" She faked a smile. "I don't know what came over me." She paused. "He's older anyway."

"When we're in court tomorrow, make sure nothing crazy comes over you. Do you understand what I am saying?"

"I do."

Chapter Eight

On the first floor of an old, creepy, white-washed limestone building, the arraignment was being held in Magistrate's Court. Tall, bushy green trees that lined the street peeked through the wooden windows of the courtroom. The arraignment and the prelim were to take place immediate after Breanna had been arrested and released on that last Thursday morning in June.

The courthouse sat across from Bermuda's central police station. Police bikes lined the street and officers dressed in light blue cotton short-sleeved shirts, navy Bermuda shorts, and dark knee-high socks commandeered the block. The complexity of love gone wrong on paradise-island caused the media to descend in droves to the small wooden courtroom where Lordship Hastings presided. The wooden spectators' chairs were filled to capacity. Sunshine ricocheted off the cream-colored walls and dropped ceilings of the courtroom. An olive green curtain hung behind the dais.

His Lordship Hastings would be known as Judge Hastings if we were in Philly. Dressed in a navy blue jacket, a lighter blue shirt, and the shorts of the island, he was a small-stature man with thick graying hair. He presided over the prelim only. A

Supreme Court Justice would sit for the actual trial. Hastings sat in a tall oak chair covered with red velvet cloth. A wooden plaque decorated the wall over his head, and read: *Dieu-Et-Mon-Droit*. I'd have to look that one up later.

This was a no-nonsense venue—little "pomp and circumstance." Even Breanna was dressed down, in a long black dress over a white cotton blouse, buttoned all the way to the top. She was not the dazzling fashion model beauty the media had made her out to be. She held on tightly to her father for as long as she could, until the time came for her to face the court. James was also present.

"Do you understand the charge against you?" His Lordship, the judge, said to her, in a heavy British accent, once the charges were read. She was being charged with first-degree murder, a crime punishable by life in prison.

"Yes, Your Honor." She stood up tall from her chair, as her mother had taught her to do, and paid careful attention to everything that was being said.

I watched too, as I was not yet admitted to practice in Bermuda. Walter was at the table shuffling his papers and preparing to argue on behalf of Breanna if the director of public prosecution gave us any trouble about her being allowed to leave Bermuda. Stephen also sat at the table as local counsel. He would nudge Walter if he did anything that was wrong in the foreign jurisdiction.

As I watched Breanna, I thought her an unlikely killer. Was someone else in fact there that night? But, those thoughts dissipated when I thought of Sean and Breanna making out on the beach. I doubted that anyone else was present.

His Lordship lightly hit the gavel as he proclaimed, "Very well. How do you plead?"

Her voice was low and hoarse. "Not guilty, Your Honor, excuse me, Your Lordship."

Hastings looked to the left at the prosecutor's table. With Breanna's words of "not guilty," the prosecutor had the job of proving beyond a reasonable doubt that Breanna had set out to deliberately kill Sean.

"Your Lordship," the prosecutor said, "Kevin Perry for the British Commonwealth Island of Bermuda." He bowed. As he approached Lordship Hastings, Perry's manner was far different from that day we'd met for the first time. He seemed now humble when he spoke. "We think in the interest of justice and foreign relations that this case should be placed on the expedited docket and that the defendant should remain in our jurisdiction while trial is pending."

Walter jumped to his feet. "Your Lordship, may I?"

"Mr. Paine."

Walter began, "We see no reason for the defendant to remain in the area. You have the assurance of the United States government that our client will remain accessible to your jurisdiction and will appear forthwith for trial. There is no threat of her escape from justice if she is allowed to return to her state of residence. She will be in the care of her father, a United States congressman."

Without a hint of hesitation, Hastings announced that the defendant was free to go. He asked the court clerk for an available trial date. The clerk reviewed a calendar and offered March and a date was set.

The clock had started to tick. We had roughly six months to prove her innocence or we'd watch her fry. "*Judgment day will come.*" Who said that? "*It is only a matter of time.*"

As we gathered to leave the courtroom, a few of the reporters rushed us.

"Mr. Paine?" a short, stocky, pale-blonde-haired woman asked as we were leaving. "Will your client remain in Bermuda for any length of time?"

Walter responded, "As you heard, we have a firm trial date in about six months."

I grabbed Breanna's arm and, with her sandwiched between Dirk and me, escorted her to Dirk's car. The congressman and the other members of our team followed in Stephen's car, which had been parked right behind Dirk's.

Apparently Sean's family had heard that the proceedings were today, because some of the same people I saw at Sean's funeral were standing outside of the courthouse talking to the television reporters, demanding to know, from what I could hear, why Breanna was not held for killing Sean.

"Blind justice!" someone yelled, and later I saw those same words on T-shirts worn by people standing outside of the courtroom. Serious allegations surfaced both at home and abroad that Breanna would never see the inside of a jail cell because of her daddy's status.

Felix, now on recess from Congress, booked the penthouse suite at the hotel, and a line of police officers on mopeds escorted us to the suite. We all went directly up where lunch was waiting.

"Can we get a change of venue?" James whispered in my ear.

"We've explored that option," I replied. That was the first I'd heard from him since he hung up on me a week ago. "We don't think we would be successful in arguing for a change of venue."

"You know how they do us."

I gave him a questionable look.

He pointed to his tanned skin. "*Us.* Can you file it tomorrow?"

I wasn't trying to get a rise out of him. It just seemed to happen when I said, "I would advise against it."

He turned red. "What do these people know about my sister?"

Walter, who overheard our conversation, motioned for Felix to handle his son.

Felix said, "I'm paying them good money to defend Breanna. Let them do their job, would you please, James."

"Dad, in my opinion Philly would be friendlier, more sympathetic."

I wanted things to be good between us. I was trying. "Actually, James, the sentiment is the same on both sides of the sea and we would, in all likelihood, not be successful in that motion because locale of the crime has ultimate jurisdiction. We are dealing with international law."

"What is the status of finding that cab driver?" Felix asked

"Dirk has been unable to track him down," I answered.

Felix shook his head. "What about the couple?"

"We'll take their depositions in August, but it's unlikely that their testimony would change. They say they saw Breanna rush off. They did not see Sean."

James' attention shifted to a cute young girl making an entrance into the suite. He went over to her, kissed her lightly, and invited her to have a seat.

Walter and Felix both walked in their direction as James introduced her as his wife, Charli. I was close enough to hear the exchange. James ignored my eyes.

Wife! She looked young enough to be his daughter! She was all of four feet tall in spiked heels! What was she doing wearing those heels anyway, wasn't she supposed to be pregnant? She had a plain and unassuming quality, nothing sassy or sophisticated as I had expected. Her chin wore the scar of a small burn mark, but she had an otherwise really cute face and she surely did not look pregnant. She was pretzel thin.

James looked in my direction, half smiled, and then turned to speak to his wife. He was obviously making our initial introduction from a distance. I hesitated, but then walked in their direction. James just stood without saying a word. He scratched the top of his head.

"Spiegel, this is my daughter-in-law, Charli," said Felix. "This is Spiegel Cullen, our attorney." We all stood there in a sort of circle.

She caught me looking at her scar. No longer did she smile as she said, "Hello."

"Hello." I stood on the heels of my shoes.

Charli said, "It is nice to meet you, Ms. Spiegel."

Ms. Spiegel?

She continued, "I never got a chance to thank you personally for the lovely wedding gift."

"You are welcome."

James looked at us cautiously while Walter, oblivious to the history, stood there and smiled.

"I thought that you were expecting?" I asked.

"We lost the baby."

"Aw, I didn't know, I'm sorry."

"Of course, how could you? We'll try again." She looked at James and touched his cheek lovingly.

I felt betrayed even though Charli was James' wife. "If you all will excuse me," I said, "I need to leave."

James stood still. Felix and Walter just looked at me.

"Will you be joining us later for dinner?" I asked Charli as I was leaving.

"I think so," she said.

I walked away as she was answering my question and did not stop until I was in my suite. I flopped onto the flower-covered chair in the room and stared out the terrace at the sailboats coasting in the waters. I felt paralyzed.

The phone rang and I hesitated for a moment. Was James calling? I grabbed it fast.

"Hello?"

"Hey, Sis. How did it go today?" Aliá asked.

"What a day—but pretty much as expected."

"You'll never believe what happened to me today! It is so spectacular!"

"Excuse me, please. I thought you wanted to know how my day went."

"Sorry, Sis. Do you have the trial date?"

"Yes."

"Spi? What's wrong? What happened?"

I took a deep breath and asked, "Are you sitting down? I just met *the* Mrs. Jordan."

"What! What's she like?"

"Young."

"Young? Hell, we're all young. How young?"

"Oh, I don't know. She looks like a kid."

"Did y'all talk?"

"Two words."

"I'm coming there. I don't start the new job for another week. I'll be there tomorrow."

"You have the money?" I asked.

"No. You do." She laughed.

"Give me back my credit card!" I made the mistake of letting Aliá use my card once and never got it back.

"Seriously, Spiegel, I'll go on stand-by. There's a chartered flight that leaves for Bermuda every morning at seven. And I have something so special to tell you."

"Okay. Damn! What is going on?" I asked.

"I was at Blockbusters today, walking up and down the aisles looking for a movie which no one seemed to have and walked right into Ahmir. Ahmir! Do you believe it?"

"Ahmir! What Blockbusters? What movie?"

"Forget all of that!" The only time I had heard Aliá this excited was on Christmas morning sitting under the tree opening loads of gifts. She always got the most gifts. My parents didn't just buy one gift, they brought at least four and more for little miss baby girl.

"Spiegel?"

"Yes, Ahmir." Ahmir and Aliá dated in college. She was pissed when he transferred to New York University.

"Oh, yeah. He says he has not stopped thinking about me since we broke up. Can you believe it?"

"Do you believe him?"

"Heck no, but I'm willing to listen to what he has to say."

"What is he doing in Philly?"

"A film project. Spiegel, guess what he said?"

"Girl, calm down. What? What!"

"He says he's not dated anyone seriously all this time; that he came back to Philly hoping that I would give him another chance."

"How does he look?"

"Exactly the same." Ahmir's a dark shade of chocolate like Hershey candy with slightly slanted eyes and a grand smile. "He said his twin sister didn't like any of the girls he's dated, because they wasn't nothing like me!"

"Girl, if Ahmir is there, why do you want to come here for the weekend? Hello!"

"He left for New York last night. He's going to visit his parents for a few days. I figure that I'll be back in Philly next week by the time he returns."

"But it's not vacation time for me. I am buried in paperwork."

The fax machine in my room made a noise before spitting out more case law for me to review.

"You can take a couple of days," Aliá said. "And, besides, I want to meet James' wife too."

"I only have a couple of days. I'm coming home on Sunday."

Aliá always got her way. "*I'll tell you what*, I'll come for the holiday weekend and come home with you on Sunday."

"Fine," I laughed. "Bye."

Chapter Nine

I never made it to dinner that night with James and his wife. Instead, I lit a vanilla-scented candle and took a long, hot shower, and then stared at myself in the bathroom mirror. What did James see in Charli that he did not see in me? Why her? But, by the time I stepped out of the bathroom, there he was.

James didn't bother to knock. He just came in and stood butt naked facing me. I stood still caught between the bathroom and the bedroom, wearing only a large hotel towel. We did not speak. He came forward. I stepped back. There we stood in the middle of the floor, taking in each other with our eyes. He stood confident, strong, and fully erect. Fruits of my desires. I was trembling as he led me to him and held me. I didn't fight, didn't question, could not even speak.

He turned off the light and the candlelight illuminated the room. Who was I fooling? In spite of myself, nobody else could move me like James. This must be what Patti Labelle meant when she sang, "*I'm hooked in spite of myself.*" He cupped my face gently in his hands, kissing my cheeks, my eyes, my nose, my lips. His hands and face felt warm. His familiar

Obsession scent excited me. "*I can't say no. It's sad but its true, I'm addicted to you.*" I was living her song, standing there still trembling as the towel slipped from me and slowly fell to the floor. James held me closer before he led me to the shower and turned the nozzle. He teased my nipples, taking them in his mouth while the water ran over his thick curly hair. I gently rubbed his head and thought of how I would take him in, but I was paralyzed and being pleased to high heaven.

"James." The word escaped from me so softly I wasn't even sure if I had spoken until he said, "Shusss." My body tensed, anticipating his touch. He kissed my stomach, just below the navel and I swiveled as tears ran from the corners of my eyes. "James," I said again softly. His face brushed warmly against the pieces of hair that covered me there until his lips touched the middle of me and took every ounce of my strength. I was limp. I gasped and held my breath until I released what felt like a river between my legs. I could do nothing. I was his to do with as he wanted.

He spread my legs and kissed my thighs, poking, licking, teasing, he turned me around. No one had touched me there since him. *Redboned.* I faced him now. Wrapping my legs around his waist, I climbed the rock.

We held on tight. "I love you, Spiegel," he said. As he entered me, he beeped. He beeped? We collapsed against the wall and eased down to the tub. We lay there, entangled in the essence and he beeped again as though he were a mechanical bird. Then I woke up.

The fax machine jarred me into reality.

Papers shot from the fax machine and other papers were strewed all over my bed. It was work that greeted me, not James. *A dream.* I had conked out last night with a pencil in my hand reading the cases on the "PMS" defense.

My blood boiled because James had entered my dreams. I turned to my work, pissed. One case had crumbled under my comforter. I snatched it and started reading where I had left off the night before. An ex-wife struggled with her husband, and in the process a gun went off and killed the man. The woman was suffering from severe depression and other PMS symptoms. In this case, the diminished capacity was enough to mitigate first-degree to third-degree. The PMS was classified as being so severe that it had been given another name: PMDD, or pre-menstrual dysphoric disorder.

That was one case in a million, and the defendant had both homicidal and suicidal ideations, of which Breanna so far had neither. Most people viewed PMS as a matter of self-control, because it affects some women severely and others not at all. We'd planned to hire a jury consultant to test our trial themes, but were relying heavily on Walter's expertise and he warned me to stay away from PMS. But I'd wait to see what the expert had to say.

Walter didn't know Breanna as I knew her. I knew her temper. I knew the Bermudian officials were asserting a case far different from that of an accident. I knew to garner any sympathy from a jury, we needed an element of emotional stress. Had something deep within snapped? Why not insanity? I remembered all of the defense attorneys I'd defeated in court who had tried that strategy. If Dr. Tyler supported the PMS theory, I'd go with it.

I stared at the wall. Enough. I had to get to the library to research other possible defenses successful in the jurisdiction of Bermuda. I skipped my usual morning jog and took a taxi to the library at the courthouse.

I loved Bermuda. A warm eighty-degree day welcomed me. The sun made it feel even hotter. At the library, I found an open cubicle and terminal, and grabbed from my bag the piece of paper that contained Stephen's identification numbers to get computer access to the universe of legal precedents. I typed in his number. Access denied. When I reached for my cell phone to confirm the number with Stephen, I noticed two missed calls; one was from Dr. Tyler. I called him back immediately.

He answered on the first ring. "Dr. Tyler." His voice was a cross between baritone and tenor.

"Spiegel Cullen."

He was quick to respond, "Yes, I must speak with you about Breanna Jordan. Are you available next week?"

I sat outside on the grassy lawn watching the locals walk alongside the narrow roads going to and from. Some carried towels over their shoulders, swatting flies as they went. "Yes. I do have your preliminary report and must admit I find it interesting, yet perplexing."

"We should sit down together on this one," he said soft-spoken yet confident, with a very faint English accent.

"I will be in Bermuda for the next few days."

"Yes, of course. Nice place to be. I think that I can help Breanna. But I don't think that even she is aware of the inappropriate behavior."

"What do you mean?"

"Life for Breanna is a game of manipulation, which she probably has played quite well in her life, juggling for attention."

"Does she have PMS or not?"

"The hormonal imbalance is a component to contend with. But that, in my opinion, is of lesser importance."

"How have you diagnosed PMS?"

"She actually has been keeping a regular calendar-like chart of her monthly symptoms at the request of her gynecologist. I suspect she has always had some symptoms of PMS."

"Always? For how long?" I paused. "And, don't write anything else down."

"The chart or diaries I've seen were for three months. I'd bet that the symptoms have been a regular part of her cycle."

"Have you had cases similar to Breanna?"

"Yes. She did something in the rush of the moment. I will continue to treat her but, in my opinion, she is far from insane."

Sad. Those split-second decisions—.

"We should meet before I commit anything further to writing." He paused. "As you requested."

"Why don't I call you as soon as I get back to Philadelphia."

"That would be fine. I want to help, Ms. Cullen. I think she is a nice young woman who has had some bad breaks in life."

"Thank you, Dr. Tyler." I hung up.

I sat for a moment, staring at the pale tourists taking pictures of the library, and tried to digest what Dr. Tyler said. I had to get her diaries to make sure she hadn't said anything about killing Sean. No intent. This would discredit their assertion of murder one. However, we now had an official position to confirm PMS. Tyler said that PMS was "a component to contend with." What did that mean? I had to find out more from the good doctor. If I could get him to state that PMS caused an emotional blackout, I'd have a good shot at developing this line for the defense.

By the time I climbed the stairs to get back to my cubicle in the library, I saw the back of someone at my cubicle, reading my papers. At first I thought it was Dirk. He was very tall and well built. But, as I got closer I could tell the man was not Dirk. I didn't know who he was. He wore black pants and a black shirt. I started to yell until it hit me that it looked like the same guy that was following me on the beach. Who was that? I slowly walked in his direction. Where was security when one needed it?

"Hey!" I yelled. The guy continued to rummage through my papers. "Hey!"

He turned quickly, and started toward me. His angry face was familiar. His voice escalated with every step. "You bitch."

I ran away from him, yelling, "Call police! Help! Somebody!"

The guy was down the stairs and out the front door before I got the attention of the security guard.

I rushed back to determine if the guy stole any of my notes, but all of my papers seemed to be in order. I packed up as fast as I could, and hailed a taxi back to the hotel.

I was so frazzled when I got into the taxi that I had forgotten the name of the hotel. I fumbled in my purse for some reminder. The driver turned to look at me from his front seat. "Are you here on the American-girl case?" The taxi driver knew of me.

"How do you know that?"

"I brought you to the hotel that night." I looked at the man, remembering him from the night I switched hotels a week or so ago. "Also, Dirk is my buddy. Shall I take you to Elbow Beach?" Dirk had so many buddies. He knew everyone on the island.

"Elbow Beach Hotel, yes, thank you."

I collected my thoughts on the way back. Dirk was there in the lobby.

"Dirk. I think that someone is following me."

"Sit down. Let me get you a drink."

"I was at the library and saw someone going through my papers."

"Are you sure?"

"Yes. I think it was the same person I saw on the beach the other morning."

"The beach?"

"Yeah . . . out on my morning run."

"What did the person look like? " He paused and grabbed me by the shoulders.

"I could be working too hard . . . but the guy did come toward me."

Dirk dropped his hands. "Not a suitor? The island is pretty safe . . . we don't have much trouble. But, I will have someone keep an eye on things around here, discreetly."

I looked into his concerned dark eyes. "Any luck?"

"With the cabby?" he asked.

"Yeah."

"I spoke to the guy's wife. She said, her husband 'doesn't want no part of the law.' He may be in some kind of trouble himself."

"Do you think that you can get him to talk with me?"

Dirk hesitated and then smiled, "I told his wife to have him call me but the Rooster . . ."

"What?"

"He wouldn't be a good witness."

"He saw something that night."

"He doesn't know what he saw."

"What do you mean?"

"King Rooster was wasted."

"Wasted?"

"Drunk."

"I'd still like to speak with him myself."

Dirk brushed his tongue over his upper lip. "How is Breanna?"

"She could be doing a whole lot better, but she's okay." I paused and then asked anyway, "Your reason for asking?" He had obviously turned his head toward Breanna.

"She's nice, is all."

"*Uh-huh.*"

"And . . ."

"And what?" I waved my hand for more.

"And, I hear Philly is nice in August."

"Philly is hot in August." I hesitated. "Are you seeing anyone, Dirk?"

"No, not really." He smiled. "Anyways, I'd like to help her."

"Can you find King Rooster?"

"I'm on it."

"Good."

Chapter Ten

"Knock-Knock!" I heard, then boom-boom went the knock at the door. "Open up the door. Let me in"

"Am I supposed to say who's there?" I joked while opening the door of my hotel room to greet Aliá.

"I made it!"

"Of course you made it!" We fell into a chair and giggled like two little girls. "I am *so* glad to see you."

She bounced in the chair. "What's up first? Bermuda!"

"I have a meeting with Stephen, first. As I told you missy-missy, not much vacation time for me."

"Aw, holiday weekend, hello. I've come to party!"

"Oh, boy."

"I'm going to put on that black sheer Kenneth Cole top I showed you—the men here—*Ooowweee*, Ohmygosh!"

"You are too crazy, okaay!"

We laughed and shook our heads.

"Where is she?" Aliá changed the subject.

"She who?"

"You know. I want to *see* everybody—James, Brea, and of course the *mizzes*."

"Girl, you not wrapped too tight. Breanna and her dad left right after the hearing. I have not seen James lately. "What's that you're reading?"

Aliá knew me far too well though. "Don't try to change the subject," she said, and tossed the book on the bed. "*No Easy Place to Be* . . . it's about three sisters."

"Any good?"

"One sister is lesbian, another passing for white, and the third is maybe the super-responsible, down with Marcus Garvey one, all growing up during the Harlem Renaissance, the Roaring Twenties. You can read it when I'm done."

"I have no time to read," I said pointing to the dark circles under my eyes.

"You used to read at night before you went to bed, no matter how tired you were."

"Not anymore."

Aliá unzipped her luggage and began hanging her clothes in the closet. "And, what's with your hair? I see gray!"

"Liá?" I screamed. "Cut it out."

"What?" She bounced about the room. "Please, can I color your hair?"

"Girl, you don't know anything about coloring hair and I don't have time."

"Make time. Let's do a cinnamon brown. It would look so pretty with your complexion."

"I'll make an appointment with Frank to get my hair done as soon as I get back to Philly."

She flopped on the bed. "You promise?"

"Promise. Now, can we get serious for a moment?" Before I knew it, the words were out: "I think someone is following me."

"What!"

"I was in the library yesterday and someone came at me, yelling. I caught him ruffling through my papers." I paused. "And, I think I saw this same guy following me on the beach."

"Yelling what?"

"I think he called me a bitch."

"What!" She stopped. "Did you tell the police about it?"

"That is part of what I am going to speak with Stephen King about."

"Stephen King—what a name for a lawyer!" Aliá stood and grabbed her purse. "We are going to the po-lice."

"No. Let me talk to Stephen first. I don't want to bring any more attention to this case than necessary."

"I still can't believe it," Aliá said. She turned to stare out of the window in an effort to hide the concern on her face. "Brea is in this shit. It was an accident. Isn't that an open-and-shut case?"

"I'm afraid not. It seemed clear that she caused his death."

"It was an accident, though." Aliá flopped back down on the bed.

I sat next to her. "But not an open-and-shut case."

"You are a good lawyer, Spiegel."

"Thanks, Sis. What are you going to do until I get back?"

"I'm going with you."

"I'll be fine. I'll be back two hours tops."

"Okay. I'll see if I can find James."

"Aliá, not a word to anyone about what I told you."

She nodded. "I'll check the schedule and have a to do list ready by the time you get back."

When I got to Stephen's office, he reported the incident at the library to the police. I left feeling ill at ease.

Aliá, as promised, was waiting in the lobby when I returned. She had bus schedules, ferry schedules, and other pamphlets on island attractions. "Do you want to tour the island by bus or ferry?"

"I don't know. I bet the ferry would be fun."

She spread out a color map of the island. "But there is a bus leaving in ten minutes to the beaches on the south side."

We hopped on bus number seven, a bus about half the size of any we'd seen in the city, and very clean and bright. The air conditioning was on full blast. Cold on the inside, the bus was pink with navy blue trim on the outside. It seated only twenty-five people and was half full, mostly with sunburned folks with cameras. At every stop, more folks enthusiastically jumped on the bus with cameras dangling from their necks. A couple jumped aboard, both wearing white shorts and matching tops, and my heart dropped to the floor.

"Spiegel, isn't that Craig?"

"I'll be damned!" My mouth hung open.

"Spiegel!" Craig jumped a step back. He turned from the cash box and headed toward the back of the bus, his complexion slowly turning flushed.

"Isn't this some shit?" Aliá said.

"Aliá, cool it," I whispered.

I looked directly at him, and he at me, as he attempted to offer some stupid introduction of his pretty and perky high school buddy. Her skin was clear and probably fair were it not for the tan. Her brown-blondish streaked hair was cut short, tapered on the sides and pixy-like in the middle. She was chubby and all of five feet six.

"Nice to meet you—Craig has told me about you," the full-figured version of Halle Berry said.

"Sorry I can't say the same. What did you say your name was again?"

"Yolanda."

"Spiegel, come on, you remember I told you I would be in this area with a friend from high school."

Aliá stood and scanned Craig and his friend from top to bottom with sheer disapproval. "What a stupid fuck," Aliá whispered. She never did care much for Craig. "*Y'all gone make me lose my mind—up in here, up in here,*" Aliá sang the tune from DMX. "*Y'all gone make me act a fool—up in here, up in here,*" she continued singing. "Spiegel, let's get off of this bus before somebody gets hurt."

In the heat of the moment, the bus jerked violently. Yolanda turned and then screamed, as the bus careened off to the side of the road and crashed through the manicured bushes. A guy on a moped was headed straight for the front of the bus. The bus swerved to the right on grassy terrain, jerking and weaving. The crash of crumpling metal came from underneath the bus.

Craig ran to the front of the bus, but the doors were closed, crushed against the bushes—no way out. The accident provided a hectic place for conversation among the four of us, or should I say the three of us, because Aliá was beyond talking. She just wanted to curse someone out.

"Spiegel, are you okay?" Craig asked.

"I'm fine, Craig." Everyone flew to the window. I expected to see blood coming from beneath the bus. The whole thing unfolded before my eyes but it was like watching a motion picture and I wasn't sure what I had witnessed. The guy on the moped had jumped off a split second before the bus hit his moped. The moped crumpled beneath the bus, but unbelievably the driver was okay.

"Must be a tourist," said one of the passengers.

"No, a local," said the bus driver, who was unshaken and calm. Seemed everyone on this island knew each other. The driver spoke to the man through her window. He was limping but otherwise okay. A few people on the bus held their backs, arms, and heads.

"Yolanda." Craig turned and asked if she were okay. They had a very easy, friendly way with each other.

"I'm okay, baby," she replied.

I was fuming. Did she just say "baby?"

"Spiegel, where are you headed?" he asked.

"None of your damn business," Aliá finally addressed Craig.

"Spiegel, I wasn't sure if you were even still here."

"I tried to call you, Craig. Did you not get my messages?"

"Listen, we are staying at the Grotto Bay."

We? I rolled my eyes hard at Craig.

He came over and whispered in my ear, "Spiegel, this is not what you think." Yolanda walked to the front of the bus.

"Craig," I attempted to keep my manner, "we are obviously not on the same page."

"What do you mean, Spiegel? Yolanda is just a friend. Where are you staying? Can we all get together for dinner?"

"Hell, no." The words came out of Aliá's mouth fast. "It is none of your damn business where we are staying."

Craig stood still, rubbing the side of his disappearing red hairline. "Spiegel, where are you headed now?"

"None of your business," I huffed. "Aliá is right about that."

The rescue and police squads arrived and positioned the bus so that the door was able to open. Only a few people were removed and taken to the hospital in an ambulance. The bus driver got up, stretched, got the bus back on the road, and proceeded along as if this were all routine stuff. The mood was still pretty excited, but after a few stops things calmed down.

When the bus driver announced Horseshoe Bay Beach, Yolanda looked for Craig's attention in the back. "Spiegel, I am going to call. Okay, baby?" he said.

"What a stupid fuck!" Aliá was saying all the words that I was definitely feeling, but felt too overwhelmed to express. As Craig and Yolanda jumped off of the bus and waved good-bye to us in a friendly bon-voyage fashion, I felt sick.

"Save yourself!" Aliá said. We arched our backs, placed one hand on our foreheads and one hand in back of our heads, took a deep breath, and laughed. "Forget him! For him to come to Bermuda with another woman, that is a bit too much. Don't you think so, Sis?"

"He said she's an old friend from high school. She lives somewhere in Chicago. I think they're just friends." I looked out the window. "He's invited us out tonight."

TICK TOCK / 95

"We have plans. Please!" Aliá stammered. "We are not going anywhere with that damn idiot and his high school sweetheart, no doubt."

"Do you mind if we head back? I don't think that I am quite up for sightseeing anyway."

"Sure, let's walk back to where Craig and Yolanda got off and join them at the beach, *shall we*. I've not been in a fight in a long time. I'm overdue."

"With all this excitement I want a drink," I added. "We can go to the beach tomorrow."

We cruised back on a sightseeing tour bus to the hotel. Dirk had left a message confirming that he would pick us up at seven-thirty that night for dinner.

I fell on the bed, kicked my sandals off, and closed my eyes in disgust. I was buried in work everywhere I turned, while Craig was having fun in the sun with someone else. I tuned Aliá out as she mumbled and grumbled about kicking Craig to the curb. Finally, she went down to the pool to do whatever. She was pissed and I was exhausted.

While I changed into something more comfortable, she doubled-back and tapped on the door only a few seconds after she had left. Only, it wasn't her at the door.

"Craig? What are you doing here?"

"I didn't feel right about what happened." He stood there for a second before he entered. "I wanted to come and see you."

"I really do have plans. What time is it?"

"Just six. What time do you have to split?"

"I should be getting ready now."

"Now?" He grabbed me tightly and brought his face to mine. "I don't want you to get the wrong impression of Yolanda."

He gripped me tightly. I was torn but let him hold me. He began to kiss the side of my neck and I backed away. How *dare* he come to my room. This was not a dream, but I said nothing.

He loosened the string of my bikini and brought me closer to him as he led me over to the bed. "Come on, Spiegel. Let me hold you. I've really missed you." *The lie unchallenged that became a truth.* "You are always so busy."

You just can't come in here and be with me while Yolanda is somewhere waiting for you, I told him off in my mind's eye. My actions were doing something completely different.

He kissed me. His breath consumed me. "Pleasures?" he asked. He knew my perfume as well as my weak spot.

I didn't kiss him back. My mind was still racing back to the bus scene when he and Yolanda got on, looking like the happy tourist couple. My body was tight. I wanted some damn answers—but not now, as he lowered his head to kiss me like a pussycat licking its kitty. I relaxed. "I've missed you, baby," he whispered.

"I've missed you too, Craig," I said as he caressed me passionately. I told the nagging voice inside my head demanding that I throw Craig's ass off the balcony to shut up. I kissed him back wildly, trying to erase every lingering thought of his travel companion.

"Oh, baby," he moaned and I thought of James, pretended he was James until Craig said, "Ooooh. Wait. Don't move. Don't move. I can't hold it. I am going to explode." And, explode I guess he did, all over himself. He hadn't even gotten his penis out of his pants. "I'm sorry, baby. I didn't want to come yet," he said as he hit the bed with a fist in a childlike manner.

"I enjoyed it, Craig. No need to apologize," I lied.

"Can I come back over later? I have a gift for you."

"How long are you going to be here?"

"We leave tomorrow." Funny, the mention of the little word *we*, brought back the dissatisfaction in our relationship. "You and Yolanda?"

"I can come back, Spiegel, and spend some time with you."

"It's over, Craig." I was serious. *Didn't need no idiot, ding-a-ling, suppose to be lover, stressing me out.*

"Spiegel! Wake up!" Aliá knocked. "Dirk is downstairs, open the door."

I jumped in the shower to rinse off and motioned for Craig to leave. He stood there perplexed for a moment. "Who is Dirk?" Aliá stopped knocking when I didn't answer. Hopefully she thought that I had left the room already. I answered Craig, "One of the investigators on Breanna's case. What do you care?"

I dressed and headed toward the door while Craig paced the floor.

"When can we talk?"

"Would you like to join us for dinner?" I asked sarcastically.

Craig looked at me with a blank stare.

"I'll call you," I said and closed the door behind him and hurried to catch up with Dirk and Aliá.

They were waiting for me at the Seahorse Grill, right on the beach. Lots of round tables were wedged in the sand with bright blue-and-white striped umbrellas overhead.

Dirk leaned back in his chair, telling a corny joke. He and Aliá hit it off right away. He said that Aliá was the fire and I the ice. When he looked up at me that night though, he looked like he had just lost his dog.

On our last night before flying back to Philly, Dirk, who had been working very had on the case, dropped a bombshell. He had been searching the island like a madman for King Rooster.

"Spiegel, sit down, relax for a moment," he said. I sat down. "The Rooster is dead."

"What? How? Dead?" My suspicion to pin this crime on someone else faded and our time was running out.

"The police found him in his cab careened off a side road in a ditch, near some construction."

"Dead?" I repeated. He was the only hope we had to place someone other than Breanna at the scene of the crime.

"What now?" Dirk asked.

"'Kiss my dick,' as Walter would say."

Chapter Eleven

M_y plane landed in Philadelphia on Sunday evening at midnight. I got home okay but worked almost until the sun came up. I'd slept for only three hours before the alarm clock put me in the ritual motions of preparing for Monday morning. Still desperately seeking anything to get Breanna off the hook, I was scheduled to speak with more of her friends.

When I walked through the doors of my office, my secretary greeted me. Ola, short and sassy like my mother, was the best legal secretary ever. I was lucky she had accepted the offer to come with me when I joined Walter. She kept me organized.

"It is going to be some day," Ola said, and handed me a stack of telephone messages. "Did you run this morning?"

"No, didn't get a chance. I was up late. Who's first?" I asked, and Ola handed me a typed list of names, dates, and times with the heading *Interview Schedule* at the top of the paper.

"Breanna's roommate for the past four years," she said.

"Okay."

My office was starting to look like I belonged there. My secretary had placed my degrees and pictures of my favorite book covers on the walls. "Do you really think this one will actually go to trial?" Ola stood in front of my desk and asked.

"It looks that way." I stood and held out my hands. "Do you have the research from John on PMS?" John was a first-year associate also assigned to this case.

"He called," Ola said. "It will be on your desk by noon. He has been in the library for the past twenty-four hours, still trying to find cases for you." Ola turned to leave but stopped. "How are you feeling? You look tired but your tan is *banging*."

"I stopped at the store this morning to get some of those one-a-day vitamins."

"All you need is a good man and some magnets. Here, I want you to wear these in your shoes for awhile." She reached over and removed her shoes and took out two insoles. "They're magnetic insoles. They'll keep your energy up." Ola was a self-proclaimed health nut. "When is the last time you had a physical?"

"I can't rightly remember," I said and shrugged, then put the insoles into my shoes.

"What's up with you and Craig? He's the *one*, Ms. Cullen. He's tall, brown, and round. What else do you need?" Ola had been my secretary for almost ten years and knew all too well the dramas of my life.

"Round?"

"Nice, tight round butt." She winked. "Did you catch up with him in Bermuda?" Ola had no intention of returning to her desk. She took a seat in the chair opposite my desk.

"Yeah, talk about drama." I could not even bring myself to tell her that Craig's buddy was a high school sweetheart.

"Was he there on business?"

"No."

"He flew all the way to Bermuda to be with you?"

"No. He and a friend came for a few days."

"That's strange, though."

"What?" I asked cautiously.

"Two guys in Bermuda. What's up with that? I know what E. Lynn Harris would say," she joked.

"Girl, puh-leeze. It's a female buddy." There, the cat was out of the bag. No taking the words back, even though I didn't want to have that conversation with Ola right then.

"Has that fool lost his mind?" She was on her feet in front of my desk, frowning hard.

"Uh-huh."

"Spiegel, I don't know about that mess."

The telephone rang and Ola answered it at my desk, "Spiegel Cullen's office."

I motioned for Ola to take a message.

"She's in depositions today, Mrs. Cullen. Can I give her a message?" My mother. I hadn't seen her since Mother's Day—several weeks ago already. I needed to get over there.

"All right, take care. Have a good day." Ola followed my every move with her eyes as she hung up the receiver. "She says she wants you to stop by this evening for dinner." Ola left and peered in the doorway a few minutes later. "Excuse me, Spiegel, Mr. Gary Jones is here." Her round face lit up. Mr. Jones was no doubt good-looking.

"He's early. We were expecting Stefany Fattah first."

"Yes, he said he doesn't mind waiting." Ola smirked. "Spiegel, Mrs. Fattah is also here," she added.

I grabbed my legal pad and headed for the waiting area to greet Mrs. Fattah. I asked Mr. Jones to wait in an adjoining conference room.

"Mrs. Fattah, thank you for coming."

"It is the least I could do," said this stunning girl. She wore a black Calvin Klein Capri pants suit with a low-cut white tank top with black trim. She pulled off both a conservative and sexy appearance. She'd make a good witness if based on looks alone, I thought, anxious to hear what she had to say.

"Why don't you have a seat." I extended my hand toward the conference room we called the fish bowl. The walls were windowed from floor to ceiling with a direct view of a big yellow clock as round as the moon atop City Hall.

"I see Gary is here also," she said and ran her fingers through her long dark straight hair.

"Yes." I offered her coffee, soda, or juice once comfortably seated in the conference room. "You know Gary?"

"That's the guy she *should* have been with. Sean and Breanna were bad news."

"What do you mean?"

Mrs. Fattah was articulate and did not waste words. "A lot of guys liked Breanna." She took a sip of her soda. "Once she met Sean, she dropped most of her friends. Sean would stay at our apartment so often, I told her either he goes or I go." She puckered. "Well, I moved out."

I played with the rubber band on my wrist. "Are you still friends with Breanna?"

She shook her head. "Sean fooled Breanna, but he didn't fool me. He had plenty of women. I'd go out and see him at the clubs with lots of different women. I tried to tell Breanna, but she accused me of being jealous. So I just stopped telling her." She paused. "Like I need to be jealous," she said, swaying her slender neck.

"What type of work do you do, Stefany?"

"I'm a dancer with Philadelphia Dance Academy."

"Is that your only job?" I asked, assuming she would have a *real* job to support her dance hobby.

"When I am not touring with the company, I teach dance."

I assumed wrong. Dancing *was* her real job. "How long have you known Breanna?"

"We met four years ago. She was dating Gary, the guy waiting out there." She gestured toward the receptionist area with well-manicured hands. "I was dating Gary's best friend. They were both on the bench for the Birds. We got along so well that we decided to room together. But, like I said, she met Sean, and Gary was somewhat history."

"Somewhat?"

"Yeah, Gary traveled a lot and liked women too, so Breanna just dealt with him when she wanted to, basically to make Sean jealous. She would call Gary whenever Sean would make her mad. Once she threw Sean out and he was gone for a week. Breanna was beside herself. She rarely slept or ate. She lost ten pounds riding all over the city, looking for him. When she found him he was living with his old girlfriend or fiancée or whatever." Stefany paused long enough to toot up her mouth and stare me in the eyes. "She's a piece of work too, you know."

"The girlfriend?"

"Yep."

"What happened then?"

"Breanna threw a brick through the window and threatened to kill herself if Sean didn't come out. He came out and calmed her down. He brought her home and stayed the night. I heard them in her bedroom acting like a happy newlywed couple." She took a swig of her soda. "He kept dealing with his fiancée. Breanna knew it. I moved the heck out."

"You mentioned that Sean's fiancée was a piece of work," I said, flipping a pencil. "Can you get into that a little bit?"

"Just that—she'd come to our apartment raising hell a few times herself, threatening to kick Breanna's ass if she didn't leave Sean alone."

I finished up the interview more perplexed than when I started. I thanked Mrs. Fattah for coming and asked if I could call her with any follow-up questions. I didn't know whether we would call her as a character witness, however, the prosecution had scheduled a laundry list of depositions into September. I wanted to meet these people prior to their depositions. I wanted to hear what they had to say. Bermuda was on a crusade to see Breanna behind bars.

The interview with Gary went well. He cared deeply for Breanna, maybe even loved her. We could count on him to be a good character witness. He didn't really have much to say other than he was aware that Breanna and Sean had been having troubles. He actually had spoken with Breanna the night before, so he knew that she was regaining her sense of reality.

After the interviews, I tidied up my office and headed to my folk's house. On the way, I grabbed lemon pound cake from the bakery downstairs to go with whatever Mom was fixing. I managed to get there by six and my father was in his usual spot, watching or sleeping through the news. I couldn't tell which one. My dad didn't work as hard as he used to; after years of running a funeral parlor, he let the younger morticians take over.

It always felt good being home for dinner. I had a sense of calm, the way things were when we were growing up. My bedroom was still pretty much the way I had left it almost twenty years ago. The outfits I wore; the books I read; the photos of friends at the time—all there in place. Home.

The thick scent of collard greens hit my nose as soon as I walked in the door and I instantly smiled. Mom made the best collards, cooked slow with smoked farm-raised turkey.

"Hi, Dad," I said.

"Where you been?" he asked and his face lit up as he swirled around in his chair to greet me. His lanky body stretched over the recliner. Aliá colored his hair a year ago and the gray had all returned. I myself thought the gray looked good with his honey brown complexion but—.

"Working hard. Is Aliá home yet?" Aliá still lived at home, the lucky girl. My mom cooked, cleaned, and generally made her life care free.

"No. She's with *that* Ahmir boy." He stayed in Aliá's business.

"Where is Mom?" I asked before I heard the rustling of keys at the front door and Mom coming through the vestibule.

"Hi, baby." She gave me a kiss. Mom's kisses sometimes felt cursory—that day was no exception. She'd never admit it, but I think she loves Aliá more. Mom was surprised but elated to have another baby girl almost twelve years after her first. Mrs. June Cullen took good care of herself however. She looked more like my sister than mother even though her roots were gray. Her skin was flawless—and a beautiful shade of caramel.

"Baby, you have any clothes of your own?" Dad said as Mom showed off my Dad's T-shirt from college, West Virginia State.

"Oh, shut up, Lewis. You ain't just now seeing me in this shirt." She turned back to me. "You all right? It looks like you've lost a little weight. Are you losing weight? Are you pushing yourself too hard?"

"I'm fine, Mom. I'm hungry."

"Good. I've made your favorite—smothered chicken, greens, and macaroni." My mom fried chicken golden brown after it marinated overnight in her special seasonings, and then she added onions, water, a smidgen of something she called kuzu which was, she said, a natural substitute for white flour, and placed it on a low fire to simmer. It was oh-so-good.

"Here's dessert." I held up the lemon pound cake and she smiled and pointed me to the cake dish. "Where's Aliá?"

"I can't keep up with y'all anymore. We have to call in advance to get you to come to dinner." Mom and I moved together through the dining room to the kitchen. "Thanks, baby for the cake," she said. "Is everything okay? How is Breanna?"

"I don't know."

"Have you spoken to that father of hers?" My mother never minced words for people she didn't particularly care for. Felix was on that list. "I always said that fool should have told that girl that her mother had taken a turn for the worse instead of letting her waltz into an empty hospital room. What kind of thing is that to do to a child?"

"I remember."

"I can't stand him. And, why hasn't he remarried in all these years—out there whoring around." My mother was just getting started. "No wonder that child is crazy."

"Mom!"

"Poor thing loses her head over and over again." Mom shook her head. "Lord knows I tried to teach her like I taught my girls how to keep your head on straight even when things were in a spin." She barely paused. "Do you think she got angry and went too far?" Mom bounced around the kitchen preparing dinner. "What do you have to do to get her off?" Her arm hung in midair, holding the grated cheese for the macaroni as she waited for me to answer.

I wished it were that easy. "I have interviews and depositions scheduled from now until September. I'm working on it."

"Now, what's up with you? Are things between you and Craig going anywhere?" she asked with an amused smile.

I knew she meant were we planning a wedding and kids, so I simply responded, "In time." No need to get her blood pressure up with my drama. Craig had been calling, six calls just last night; four the night before begging for me to call him back. *Nope.*

"There is a nice young man at church, Spiegel. Why don't you come with me to church. . . ." Her voice trailed off as I attempted to respond, but she wasn't finished. "Father Haskel would be so pleased to see you as well." She went on thinking and plotting in her mind until she reached some subconscious conclusion that made her smile.

I smiled just watching her.

"Dinner is ready," she yelled to my Dad, and that conversation both real and imagined came to an end.

Chapter Twelve

Late August, then early September, had come and gone. Wind whipped in a sunny, but chilly September morning. A day aching beauty, the leaves had already begun to fall, bursting in shades of burnt orange and yellow. We'd completed depositions of people close to Breanna, but nothing good came out. Breanna was in quicksand.

I'd looked to Tyler to help me figure her out, and came to enjoy our chats even though we had not yet met. He'd continued to see her weekly and reported that she was in much better shape—unlike when she performed the unauthorized strip tease, now almost three months ago. I was looking forward to hearing what Tyler had to say, but first couldn't let a day filled with clear skies and sunshine escape without a jog.

Typical Saturday, lots of people were out jogging despite the chilly wind. I trotted off at a snail's pace once out my front door, until my body caught up with the voice inside my head that got me up this morning. Running puts me in a balanced place. My legs were aching, though. If I had gone any slower, I would have damn near been walking.

"Spi?"

I turned hastily to greet my nosy neighbor, Shelia. She took mood swings to a new level. She was smiling this day. Other days she'd look at me and not even speak.

"Hey, girl," I said, still trying to catch my breath but kept running down the hill to the Drive.

"Hi, I've not seen you since the Mother's Day race." Her micro-braids were swirled in an up-do loosely held in place with a yellow hair clip. "Did you have a good Mother's Day?" she said with a forced, embarrassed smile when it hit her that I'm not a mother. "Or, should I have said, a Happy Auntie's Day?" She smiled.

"I have to go." I meant to be abrupt. Mother's Day was a while ago. I couldn't even understand why she brought it up. I looked at her with a weird expression.

"I still have a card for you. I've had it for months."

"Stick it in my door," I said with a dismissive giggle.

"Spiegel. I know you've been busy. Where did you go to law school again?"

We ran side by side like running buddies along the dirt path near a tranquil river. "Temple."

"*Oh*, I thought you went to *Penn*."

"Penn as an undergraduate," I corrected.

"Perhaps I can talk to you about it when things settle down for you. I'm thinking of going back to school. How is your case going with the girl in Bermuda?"

"It's going."

"Oh, did that detective catch up with you the other day?"

I stopped. "What are you talking about?" The geese began to quack in the water as a canoe of college students rowed up river.

She stopped too. "There was a guy at your door the other day. I watched him through the window for a while because he stood at your door for so long, and it was obvious that you were not at home. I mean no lights, no car, and no answer at the door. Yet, he just stood there."

"When?"

"The other night. I think maybe it was Thursday."

"What did he look like?"

"Average looking, big guy."

"Black? White?"

She wiped her forehead. "Black guy, dark, big smile. I thought for sure he left a card or something in the door."

"No."

"I'll check at home. Maybe he gave the darn thing to me. I think I scared him a little when I walked over to tell him that you weren't at home. I'll let you know as soon as I get home if I have his card."

"Thank you."

We doubled back and ran at a slow pace the rest of the way through the Sycamore and Slippery Elm trees up a steep hill to our homes. By the time I ate something and got out of the house, the mailman was on his four o'clock round.

Dr. Tyler's office was all the way out in Ft. Washington, an affluent suburb near Philadelphia. He had agreed to meet me on a Saturday. When I arrived, the door was open so I walked into the waiting area. The office was small and uniquely decorated, reflective of a person who traveled extensively. Trophies from running competitions sat on top of a corridor table. A runner? He appeared from one of the other offices.

"Please come in. Spiegel Cullen. I finally get to put a face to a voice." The first thing I noticed about him was his jet-black dreadlocks pulled back into a ponytail. His color was brown, almost bronze, rich, and smooth. He was not that tall, maybe five feet seven, but firm and well built. He smiled and his thick dark mustache accentuated his full lips.

"Yes, likewise."

He moved around his office with ease. "Would you like something to drink?" The second thing I noticed was a diamond stud earring in his left ear. He didn't fit the image of someone so accomplished. "Coffee would be fine."

"Give me a second. I'll have to dig the coffee out. I mostly drink tea."

"Tea?"

I didn't notice a wedding ring, not that I was looking for a ring or the absence of one. I did notice his eyes, however. They were dark brown, warm and inviting but not flirtatious. His brows were thick like his mustache.

I'd like to lie down on that couch and tell him my troubles, but said a gracious, "Thank you," as he handed me the coffee and escorted me to his office. Painted a soft ivory, his office was simply furnished with his desk and swivel chair, a sofa and a loveseat for visitors. Bookcases and colorful pictures of oceans, mountains, and skies hung on his walls. I immediately felt warm and comfortable. One picture in particular of an empty beach chair facing an ocean was hypnotic. I pictured myself comfortably seated in that chair daydreaming of living a life of leisure. What did his home look like? He even had Billie Holiday playing softly in the background and a green apple-scented candle burning.

"Ms. Cullen, we have an interesting situation here in Breanna Jordan."

I went for my coffee while he pulled a file from his desk and scanned through it. "Has she kept her weekly visit with you?" I asked.

"Oh, yes. Her father, though her brother now that Congress is back in session, brings her regularly. Felix is a personal friend of mine."

Who wasn't a friend of Felix's? I had read Tyler's bio and knew that he was much younger than Felix. At forty-eight, Dr. Michael Tyler had a youthful appearance. He had achieved acclaim in the psychology profession on staff at the University of Pennsylvania for eleven years before going into private practice. He had published works in prominent medical journals, delving into the psychology of people who kill. *Lady Day* played on in the background. *I fell in love with you the first time I looked into them there eyes. . . ."*

"Dr. Tyler, do you see any progress in Breanna? You mentioned previously that she knows the difference between right and wrong and is competent to stand trial."

"Yes, I don't see any real evidence of mental disorder. I want to help her in spite of her continued inappropriate behavior."

"The flirting?"

"Primarily."

"Has that stopped?"

"She is starting to open up with me more. She suffers from very low self-esteem."

I squirmed in my seat. "She is the picture of beauty."

"On the outside." He paused and leaned back in his chair. "She has a strong need to be accepted, to be liked, prompted perhaps by the sudden death of her mother, or some inability to receive love from those in a nurturing position as she was growing up."

"Are you talking about her father?"

"Could be."

"If that was the case, then there must be a whole lot of people out there with low self-esteem."

"Achoo!" he sneezed.

"God bless you," I said.

"Thank you. As I was saying, yes, but we don't go around killing our mates. I suspect that there are underlying feelings of rejection, isolation, and perhaps unresolved issues stemming from her mother's death. I think you lawyers call it mitigating circumstances."

"All of the mitigating circumstances I come up with still don't tell me why."

"Why?" Tyler folded his arms. "As in why she may have in fact killed Sean?"

"It is my opinion that it was an accident; that she never meant to kill him but to hurt him, maybe. The press sees her as this dazzlingly beautiful, cold-blooded killer; a woman scorned."

"I'd look harder for the mitigating circumstances," Dr. Tyler said. "The PMS is a formidable defense."

"Again, PMS usually doesn't make you kill."

"I'm not sure my ex-wife would agree." We laughed.

"Seriously, she runs a PMS study center in Boulder, Colorado, and has consulted with lawyers on this subject before. Should you need to be in touch with her, I can reach her for you."

Ex-wife? "Is she a Dr. Tyler also?"

He stood up from behind his desk and took the chair next to mine. "No, actually she has remarried. Her name is Dr. Janelle Light."

I could picture my opening statement now, putting the case of PMS on trial. I'd be known as Spiegel Cullen, the PMS lawyer with a tag line to women every where that read: *Just do it but make sure it's that time of the month.* "I actually have a conference later this month with a Dr. Black at Temple, who also runs a study group on PMS issues."

He leaned forward on his knees. His legs were open and he continued reading from his notes, "Her medical records also reveal a slight imbalance of estrogen, which can trigger PMS. The imbalance, the symptoms, are really not severe enough, but I guess we could make a case for it if that was all we had."

The "PMS made me do it" defense may be out. Either PMS made her crazy or it was an accident, plain and simple. The latter was starting to look like the best defense.

"Do you often get immersed in your own thoughts?" he asked.

"No. Sorry."

"I'd never met with Breanna as a patient before all this happened. I'd known her as a young girl, and I recall vividly her asking me if I could bring her mother back once when I was at their home as a dinner guest." He paused and placed his hand over his heart. "She clearly still is in a lot of pain over her mother's death."

"That was over ten years ago." I stiffened my back and sat up. "Do you realize that she may be facing life in prison?"

He sat up straight as well and focused his eyes more directly on mine. "Even though it was an accident?" he asked, barely blinking when he spoke.

"Yeah, accident or no accident. I can't let that happen."

Dr. Tyler would make a good witness. Intelligent, but not condescending, he'd be good for the defense.

"Is she suicidal, doctor?"

"Her mood swings can be extreme. However, as long as she is taking the medicine she should be okay, provided she is under a doctor's care."

"How long before she's well?"

"That depends on Breanna. There are different levels of wellness. By all outward appearances, Breanna is well. Her emotional turmoil is aggravated by the circumstances. In my opinion, once she deals with the root of her pain, she will, let's say, be at a higher level of wellness."

Dr. Tyler walked me outside to my fifteen-year-old coupe; it runs, it's paid for, and the heat works just fine. It was chilly football weather. "How did you manage to get a spot right in front of the office at this time of day?" he asked.

"Luck, I guess." My cell phone rang. "Excuse me a second; I need to take this call." I spoke quickly and ended the call before extending my hand to him. "It was a pleasure meeting you." His handshake was strong and firm.

"Is everything okay?" Dr. Tyler asked and smiled.

"Yes, wrong number. Men!" I wished that I could have taken that back—no need for him to know my personal business. Why had I said that to him?

"I look forward to our next meeting," he said as he closed me in my car with a smile. *What a nice guy.*

I drove home at a leisurely pace. I phoned the office to check my calls then I pulled off the road for a quick bite to eat. The neon sign of the Holiday Inn lured me to food. The restaurant was cheerful—big-screen TV, a lively crowd starting to gather for the early dinner specials.

I ordered steak, fries, and broccoli and also welcomed the warm cinnamon apple bread. I loaded it with butter before I went for the ladies' room. On the way back to the table, I practically tripped, stumbling into the waitress escorting, to my surprise, Dr. Tyler to a table. *Ohmygod! His thick, black, wavy locks were loose. He looked like the mo'better-blues Denzel with braids.*

"Spiegel!" He grinned. "I imagine that you had the same type of lunch as I did?" he asked. "Would you mind if I joined you?"

"Not at all. Please do." I answered.

He sat down and ordered a cup of soup and crackers. "Do you often eat that much?" he joked when he saw my plate.

"No. Very funny." We laughed.

During the meal, Tyler told me that his mother was a widow and coincidentally, a Bermudian. She lived on the island near Hamilton. Tyler himself traveled to Bermuda three four times a year. "I'd like to buy a vacation property there but the treaty bill whatever is tied up in political minutia." He paused. "The real estate market is only open to residents."

I nodded.

The heavyset waitress strolled back to ask if we needed or wanted anything else and Tyler handed her the empty breadbasket.

"I see you like hot, buttered cinnamon bread also," he said.

"Yes—my weakness." A wise guy!

"You can afford it." The conversation was looking up. "You're in great shape. You can have fun with bread and butter," he said.

Dare I let me guard down? I smiled.

He was staring at me. I felt shy all of a sudden.

He smiled back. "So tell me a little about Spiegel Cullen."

"I'm a lawyer." Dah!

"No kidding, Sherlock!" We cracked up. "Why a lawyer?" He grabbed a cinnamon roll from the refilled basket and meticulously diced the butter, opened the roll, and rubbed the butter inside.

I watched his strong slender fingers and took a swig of water. I like a man with a slow hand, an easy touch. "When I was little, my friend was killed by some boys in the neighborhood. The police found her in an alley. I'd promised then to get all those bad boys."

"And now."

"And now, I'd like to help Breanna at the moment."

"Are you married?"

Was he flirting with me? I shook my head.

"Spiegel is a different sort of name?"

"Spiegel Rose actually. I was named after my grandmother."

Over tea, we finally cut to the case. He had testified in murder trials before, and believed that Breanna was telling the truth, that she did not intend to harm Sean—a position I wished I shared.

"Frankly," I said clicking my teacup and saucer, "my confidence in a PMS theory is diminishing. I'd have to prove that it was so severe that it caused her to have lost her mind."

"It'd be a stretch." He paused and raised his eyebrows. "What would you need to prove that it was merely an accident?"

"For starters, no intent and no motive." I placed my hand on my hip.

"What about her diaries?" He was on to something.

I nodded. "Bermuda wants murder one. I was a little surprised that they didn't go after involuntary manslaughter."

"What about the detective she's seeing? Has he—"

"She's seeing a detective?"

"I met someone a while back who was here visiting from Bermuda." He pondered. "Dirk I think was his name. Has he found anything?"

"No one at all." *Uh-huh. I hadn't known that Dirk had come to visit Breanna.* I started to collect my stuff. "I can drive back to your place and get the diaries so that I can review them when I get home."

"All work, no play?" He lightly touched my hand.

By the time I got home, a full moon lit my driveway. Walking up to my front door, my heart started to pound. A card or note was wedged in the door. I eased the note out gently, opened the door quickly, and rushed to lock it behind me. Someone was watching. I could just feel it.

It wasn't a card; it was a small piece of paper folded over with scribbling inside in black magic marker from my nosy neighbor. Somewhat relieved, I read the note: *Sorry Spiegel. I can't find the card from the stranger. But it may not have even been a note. What I remember is that the guy looked an awful lot like the guy they showed on television that your client murdered in Bermuda. I hope to see you soon about my applying to law school. Did you say that you went to the evening program? Shelia*

Chapter Thirteen

The case had remained status quo over the next several months, but the pace was about to pick up, as it was now November and the trial was set for spring. Someone had pushed a fast-forward button to the holidays. Dirk and the investigative team in Bermuda continued to look for new developments, but turned up nothing. Even after chasing down every exhaustive lead from friends, islanders, cops, and others, nothing. I was stressed and had not seen Craig in months.

On a whim, I called Craig back. He sounded strange, but said he wanted to stop by. For better or worse. I felt like crap. A winter cold had caught me off guard. My lips were dry and chapped. I'd been asleep for hours. I put on the kettle for tea and scrounged around to see if I had any food in my refrigerator. I crawled back into bed starved, tossing and turning from hunger. Ridiculous. I got up and ordered a pizza.

"Extra cheese, sausage, and extra sauce."

The doorbell rang shortly after I had placed the order.

Craig was at the door.

"You wear glasses?" he asked. He looked good. He stood there in the doorway while a light dusting of snow melted into his dark green, tailored wool suit.

I felt exposed. I was too sick to bother with contact lenses. "Sometimes," I said. "Is it snowing?"

"Baby, please. I've been trying to get with you for months."

Four months, three weeks and four days to be exact. "Oh." I closed the door. *Did absence make the heart fonder?*

"You sick?" He took off his suit jacket and swung it across the sofa.

"What do you think?" I said. He was acting funny, as Aliá would say, "Something wasn't right."

He put his hands in his pants pocket and circled the room with his hands still stuffed in his pockets. "I'm sorry, Spiegel." He moved closer to me. "I want you back in my life. I've spent the last few months thinking of you."

I listened.

"I never really wanted a serious relationship when we started going out," he blurted out. His face twitched with every word.

"Huh?"

"Do you want marriage or something?" He lightheartedly grinned.

I said each word slowly, cautiously. "Are you saying you want to get married?" My heart skipped a beat.

"You?" he asked.

"What about kids?" I asked. My eyes widened.

He shrugged. "You?"

"Are you saying you don't want kids?" The question now on the table, my heart was sinking. At that instant, I realized that I liked Craig more than I thought that I did. Was the feeling mutual?

"Do you want to get married?"

"Are you proposing?" I asked.

He shrugged again. "I don't want to hurt you."

"Are you proposing?" I felt pathetic.

"Can I get you something? Do you want me to run out and get you some medicine?" he asked, dishing out crap and concern in the same stroke.

"No. Did you see the game today?" His face lit up when the doorbell rang.

"Pizza," I said. "Do you have any money?"

He went to the door to get the pizza. "Do you have beer?" he asked and shook from the cold air as he closed the door.

"I think you left some in the refrigerator." He loved pizza with lots of cheese. He was content for the time being.

I awoke in the morning to hear the front door closing. Craig was leaving.

I dressed in a hurry to get into the office at least for part of the day. Did Craig ask me to marry him? Was he serious?

I called Craig before jumping in the shower to see if he was available for dinner, lunch, or something. He did not answer his cell phone. I left a message about a get-away weekend. He just needed more of my attention.

I played back the calls on my answering machine.

"Just wanted to say hello." James called twice. "When you get a moment, call me. I've been thinking about you," James said on the second call.

At ten o'clock, I strolled into the office.

"Please go home, Ms. Cullen," was Ola's request as soon as she laid eyes on me. "It does nobody any good if the entire office catches your bug."

"I'm actually feeling better." My desk was covered with neat stacks of papers and files. I took a file sandwiched between other files, marked "scene of the crime containing photos." I held the photos. "Breanna is coming in today."

"What time? I didn't see anything on your calendar," Ola said.

"Two, but would you see if she can come in now?"

"No problem."

I wanted Breanna to view the photos of the scene, including Sean's body. Up until now, she had been unable to look at the photos, but Tyler said she was ready now. She must look at his swollen body and determine if he was in the same condition as when she last saw him. I'd have to be gentle. I didn't want Breanna flipping out so close to trial.

"Would you also get James on the telephone?"

"Sure. Breanna will be here at one. Would you like coffee or something?"

"Would you mind running next store to get me chicken noodle soup and a bagel?"

"Ms. Cullen, your mom is on line one."

I picked up the phone. "Mom. I was in bed all day yesterday. Why didn't you have them take my tonsils out when I was a kid?"

She went on and on about the benefits of tonsils and insisted on bringing soup to my home that evening. "And go to your doctor and have him check to see if you have iron-poor blood. Better yet, I'll make an appointment for you with my doctor."

"I'm fine mother, but I am due for a physical." I'd go. "Love you too, bye-bye."

The telephone rang again.

"Spiegel, it's James," Ola said, poking her big head into my office.

"Hello, James," I said.

" 'Tis the season," he sang.

James and I were doing better in handling working so closely on Breanna's case. I'd started calling him periodically, keeping him in the loop.

"How's the *family*?" I countered.

"Everyone is fine. How are you?" He had learned to ignore my sarcasm. "Breanna and I are in town and was wondering if you were free for lunch."

"I'm not feeling good." I considered his request. "Can I take a rain check?"

"We are right downstairs. Can't you get away for a quick lunch?"

"Downstairs?" I held the phone, considering his request further.

"You told me never to drop in on you without calling and Breanna was coming to see you anyway."

"What are you doing downstairs?"

"Enough with the questions. I want to see you." He paused. "Come on down."

The office was quiet with lots of people on vacation or off doing holiday shopping. I told Ola that I would be meeting Breanna out of the office and would not return so if she liked, she could leave as well.

"Bet!" Ola screamed as I collected the gruesome photos and headed downstairs.

James and Breanna stood waiting near the elevator bank when I stepped off. "What the heck?" as Aliá would say "are you two doing here?"

"It was his idea, Spiegel," Breanna said, pointing to her laughing brother. Breanna looked well. She was wearing that long fur coat I'd seen her in on a sadder occasion. It looked much better on her now than it did at Sean's funeral. She carried a handful of bags from Toys-R-Us. Her hair was even shorter, closer to her scalp. If she weren't so pretty she'd look like a dude.

"Hey, Breanna." I kissed her cheek. "What have you been up to?"

"I was hanging out with Liá last night! She giggled. "We had a ball."

"Hello, lunch? Remember me?" James joked.

We both looked at him.

"Okay, where to?" I asked. I was starting to feel better. Being with Breanna and James felt like happier times when . . . well. . . .

We left my office building on Market and headed south toward Broad Street to a restaurant called Zanzibarblue. We huddled hand-in-hand to shield ourselves from the snow now starting to fall. Zanzibarblue was just a few blocks away on the Avenue of the Arts but its international jazz and French, American, and Cajun cuisine was worth the walk in the snow.

When we arrived, the lights were dimmed and jazz greats adorned the walls. A very attractive stick figure greeted us at the door and seated us near a center stage. The hostess was tall and thin with wild, but fashionable natural hair.

The stage was set for the evening performances but the place was quiet during lunch.

"So why are you sick?" James asked when we were all comfortably seated.

I couldn't shake this cold. "Why does anyone get sick?" I could always be myself with James and say whatever came to mind first. "You are a complete fool."

He laughed, then we all laughed.

"A lover's quarrel?" Breanna joked. She pulled toys from her bags showing off gifts she purchased for St. Christopher's Hospital for kids. I remembered how Breanna and Aliá loved to shop. Breanna had many bags.

"You know better," I said and turned to the menu.

"Drinks?" James asked. "It's holiday time."

"I'm taking Dimetapp. Nothing for me."

Breanna ordered rum and Coke. "Look!" she said with too much excitement, while pulling toys from the bag. "I'm going to hate to part with this one." It was a giant stuffed tweety bird. "It's my favorite."

"Anything for you, sir?" The waitress was still standing at our table, smiling at Breanna's antics.

James ordered wine. "Put that dang bird back in the bag," he said. The waitress walked away, laughing. "Isn't that guy of yours taking care of you?" James was determined to get under my skin.

I did not respond.

"He can't help it, Spiegel," Breanna chimed in. "I've got a new love, Spiegel," she said eagerly placing the toys out of the way.

"A new love?" I found myself getting an instant attitude. How could she dismiss what happened so quickly? "Do you think that's a good idea?" I asked. My mood was going downhill. Was it Dirk?

The waitress returned with the drinks then moved on to the next table.

"I have to move on. Doctor's orders," she said reaching for her drink. "We're going away for New Year's weekend."

"As in four, five weeks from now? Where?" I asked. James and I both looked at each other and then to her for a response. My eyes matched the concern he held in his.

"Relax," she said. "We're just going to New York."

"You have a trial coming up in only a few months," I said. "Be careful." I weighed pulling out the photographs to get her to confirm the condition of the Sean's body. "As a matter of fact, Breanna," I said and a chill came over our threesome, "I have some photos I need you to identify." I reached over and pulled the folder from my brief case.

"Not now, for God's sake. It's almost Christmas," James said.

"I'm okay, big brother. Spiegel told me about the photos. She wants me to look at them."

"They'll shove them in her face at trial," I told James. "She has to look at them." Up until now, we had not had much luck getting Breanna to walk the crime scene. Getting her to look at these photos was a compromise.

"Why now?" James asked.

"Why *not* now?" I demanded. I thought in this upbeat environment Breanna would be okay. But, she had second thoughts.

"I've changed my mind, Spiegel," she said, "I don't want to see the photos. I may not be able to handle it. I've already told you everything. I even drew diagrams of where we were standing."

I placed my hand on the corner of the folder as though to open it. "You have to revisit this, Breanna, over and over again so that you can handle yourself at trial. If not today, when? The prosecutor will try to tear you to pieces." I paused. "We have to be ready to handle whatever he throws at us."

"I know, Spiegel, but my dad said—"

"Lets keep your dad out of this for a minute."

Her eyes bulged. "I just want to go away for New Year's eve and have a nice time."

I placed the photos back in my briefcase and decided to try to get into the spirit of the holiday. I'd get Breanna to review the photos, but now proved not to be a good time. "Okay, Breanna. Okay for now."

We all exhaled. Breanna's free-spirited behavior made me think of planning that trip with Craig. My mood improved.

Chapter Fourteen

Craig and I finally got *away* around Christmas. We packed overnight bags and headed to Baltimore Harbor.

Craig, all proud while driving his town car, grinned. Why such a big car?

"What are you looking at me for?" I asked.

"You look nice. Can't I just look at you?" he said. "You've changed your hair." No more ribbon and bun. It was time for a change, a reddish-brown color and a blunt, straight cut to my neck. "I like it." I put my shades on and swayed my hair from my eyes. "You look like Hollywood girl!"

"Why, thank you." I had even gotten my nails and toes painted fire-engine red. I beamed, too.

"Where are we staying?" he asked and adjusted the rear view mirror.

"It will be a surprise!"

"How much is this going to cost me?"

"It will be fun!"

We arrived at the Hyatt at about one that afternoon on a crisp and clear winter day. The sun was warm and shining brightly in our room that overlooked the waves crashing against the docksides. The Baltimore Harbor Aquarium sat across the murky water, surrounded by hotels, a large sea vessel, and a shopping mall. The *Spirit of Baltimore* was anchored.

I had planned so many fun things for us to do! We set down our bags and went out on the balcony. Craig grabbed me from behind while I was looking out at the harbor.

"Merry Christmas, baby." I held his hands in my hands when he wrapped his arms around my waist, my back comfortable against his chest.

"What are you doing to me, Spiegel?" He buried his head in my neck and kissed me gently.

"What are you talking about?"

"I may be falling in love with you," he said, and I was silenced again.

"We better get started," I said, trying not to focus on what Craig just said. I had thought I'd never hear Craig say the word love—even wondered if it was in his vocabulary. When he finally said it, I had no reply. I smiled and frowned.

"Where to?" He pulled back. I turned around to face him. He raised an eyebrow.

I said, "Blacks In Wax Museum is open for another two hours. Why don't we go there first?"

"First?" He smiled a pleasing smile. "Actually that is one place I've always wanted to visit."

I could see why other women liked Craig. He had a way of going with the flow. He and I, both history majors, shared a keen interest in controversial stuff, which is one of the reasons I knew he'd be up for the museum trip.

"Craig, look at this!" I said when we entered the museum. I pointed to the wax figures of famous writers. "They look so much like Zora Neale and Richard Wright. Look! Look at Baldwin at his typewriter." The museum was filled with wax images of notable people, clad in appropriate historical attire.

We crept though the slave trade, ancient Africa, and the Middle Passage.

"Get the shit!" Craig said from the hallway staring ahead at a slave ship. Slowly we stepped onto the slave ship, where men and women were shackled and stacked like sardines in a can. My stomach tightened. Hesitantly I moved, step by step, following closely behind Craig. The women—naked, swollen, sick, some pregnant, some dead, chained together—lay amidst rats, mice, and vomit. Sorrow immediately changed my mood from one appropriate for a joyous get-away weekend to a sincere desire to flee.

"Get the shit," Craig whispered again.

What could be worse? I walked toward the exhibit on lynching. Photographs of African-Americans, hanging from trees with ropes around their necks, along the walls leading to an open door. Above the door a sign read: "Advisory: This exhibit contains sensitive and potentially disturbing scenes. Parental guidance and discretion are advised." Strange Fruit. "Southern trees bear strange fruit, blood on the leaves and blood at the root," wrote Lewis Allen. Billy Holliday sang, "Black bodies swinging in the southern breeze. Strange fruit hanging from the poplar trees."

I followed Craig through the door. On a ledge were real body parts—knees, testicles, and fingers—floating in a jar. "Is that what I think it is?" I asked.

"Yep."

"Are they real?"

"I think so." We both turned from the eyeballs floating in formaldehyde to the life-sized wax figures of a husband and wife lynched and hanging together from a tree. The wax figures of a black cat and a white cat stood underneath their dangling bodies, eating what they could reach of the couple's remains.

"Craig? Did you read this? She was pregnant. They cut the baby out of her stomach and sewed the cats in her stomach." I read on. "The tormentors stood by placing bets on which cat would claw its way out first—the black one or the white one." I was ready to go. The pain was too much.

"Get the shit."

"Do you think that they really sewed cats in her belly and took bets on how fast the cats would claw out?"

"Claw out?" He finished my question with me.

"Yeah," I said.

"Uh-huh."

No one would ever believe this. "Why do you think we didn't see that shit in the movies?"

"I hear you, baby."

I stared for as long as I was able at the fragments that remained. We were the last to leave the museum. I instantly felt that I was not doing enough to help our society.

"I can do more to make the world better," I said.

"Okay, Oprah." I went to smack Craig playfully, but he caught me and held me close to him for a while. We were getting our groove back.

"The Sixers are playing tonight," he chuckled. "Are you ready to get back to the hotel?"

I was exhausted. After taking that step into history, I felt like I had been working in a cold mine.

Back in the hotel room, we called room service for dinner. Afterward, Craig watched the game and I snuggled under the covers. I'd been so wrapped up in work, Craig may have felt a little slighted. But my application to practice in the Bermuda court had been approved, and I was scheduled to be in Bermuda most of January and February with trial prep. I tried not to think about what would happen over the next three months. The emotional tug of war was tough.

I poked my head out from under the covers to see what Craig was doing. He was so into the game he might as well have been in the room alone. I covered up again and wiggled into a comfortable sleeping position. Of all people, I thought of James before falling off to sleep.

Thunderstorms and lightening ushered in Saturday. "After breakfast, would you like to go to the movies?" I asked. I still had on my pretty-in-pink Victoria's secret sheer pajamas, and was sitting at the small round table in the room. Taking full advantage of room service, we'd ordered breakfast.

"To see what?" Craig was prancing around in his shorts. His pale chest was bare.

"The *Best Man* sounds good." We might have a "light-bulb" moment, since the movie was about relationships.

"Fine," he said. "Isn't that the one with Nia Long?"

"Yeah." I forgot about Nia Long, silly me. He'd go anywhere to see Nia Long.

By the time we had dressed and strolled around the mall for souvenirs, we had missed the matinee but were in time for the early evening show. Craig fell asleep during the movie. Afterward, we ended up at Café America, an exquisite restaurant that was at the end of the harbor set within an artistic junkyard like charm.

While passing him the bread, I whispered, "save room for dessert. I brought the sweets." I was feeling optimistic about our relationship.

"Ooh." He stopped buttering his breadstick, looked at me and flashed a grand smile.

We devoured our chicken and veal parmigiana without delay, excitedly anticipating our evening. We were going to exchange Christmas gifts.

When we got back to our hotel room, Craig tossed me a bag full of gifts while he flipped channels to find a basketball game. "Gifts for me?" I asked and sat on the bed.

He smiled.

"I can tell what these are." I shook the sneaker box before opening it to prolong the joy of opening a lot of gifts. "Reeboks! I *like* them!"

The next box was small, like a ring box. Could it possibly be? I shook the box. "Shake, Shake, Shake." Craig was so busy watching a basketball game he didn't even notice me. "What could this possibly be?"

"If you don't like it, I can take it back." He turned in my direction.

"The box is so small."

"Just like a woman . . . always looking for the big box."

I hit him playfully.

"It's what's inside that counts. Right?" Craig gave his full attention to me and I blushed and sweat. I opened the small box carefully, one corner at a time. "Open the box girl."

I did. "The earrings are nice," I lied. I felt empty inside. Did this guy even care for me at all? The earrings looked like something he'd picked up at the sale counter at Kmart. I felt chilly all of a sudden. The other gifts were just as bad—a writing pen, an organizer, and a pair of running shorts. Would now be a good time to bring up the marriage proposal?

I tossed his gift to him. He opened it right away—tickets to the Super Bowl in San Diego. "Thank you, baby!" he said and turned to the television to finish watching the game. I snuggled down under the covers of our king-sized bed alone.

He woke me after the game by parting my legs and kissing the inside of my inner thighs. I woke up smiling. I moaned. My legs tightened, but his strong arms and elbows held them open while he buried his head between my legs. I was wet immediately. I gently rubbed his bald head. When he came to me he said, "Now you do me." He playfully pushed my head between his legs. "Give *Peter* some love."

I resisted. Craig was small but skillful in the art of lovemaking. I kissed his stomach while watching *Peter* grow bigger and bigger. *Should I?* Usually, if we're not in the shower or just jumping out of the shower I don't go there. But, it was Christmas, hell.

I stroked him. He moaned a little when I slid my tongue up and down his shaft. I slid him into my mouth and sucked him hard. With each suck, my lips and nose were closer and closer to his coarse red locks. Craig grabbed the sheets with both hands. I eased back, stopping to circle the tip of his *peter.* He grabbed my head with both hands, nudging me to take him again. I did. "Damn, girl!"

I pulled up, "Turn around." I loved being a bad girl. Craig brought that out of me. He taught me how to do the freaky stuff.

"Baby, Baby, Baby," his voice escalated as he turned to lie on his stomach. Craig was confident in his lovemaking, and let me try just about anything with him. We found some sizzling spots.

I was hot and getting hotter pleasing him. I opened his strong legs and bent over to kiss his cheeks one at a time. "Oh, girl!" he moaned. "Shit, damn girl!" he hollered and his body shook. He was beyond ready to explode, but I wanted him inside of me. As soon as he turned to face me, his dick was so hard and big it actually looked painful. "Spiegel, please." He was begging now. I slid up on top of him and opened my legs wide as he easily, naturally found his way home. He grabbed my butt and thrust me to him hard, fast, and angry. Craig liked a rough climax, but he stopped short just long enough to unwrap a condom and ease it over his throbbing penis. We were monogamous—a condom?

"Baby, please don't move," he said when he was back inside. With that, our twenty minutes of blissful lovemaking—no fucking—were over. His penis shriveled back up and the condom fell off.

We kissed and cuddled most of the night before falling asleep, eventually butts touching at the tips like the greater-than and less-than math symbols.

On Sunday, he woke up smiling. We packed and hit the road back to Philly. Craig was in a rush. I slept most of the way home. I felt surreal as the sun hit my face, confident that one day we'd star in our own version of *The Best Man.*

Chapter Fifteen

Around the first of the year, the trial was rescheduled for some time in April because of a personal conflict of the judge's. That meant I had more time to work with Tyler getting Breanna ready for trial.

A few weeks prior to the trial date, I drove to Tyler's office. When I arrived, the doors to the general waiting area were open, so I walked on in. Voices came from behind a slightly ajar office door. They could not see me and I was quite sure that Tyler was not aware that the door had opened. I thought of knocking, but instead stopped and slowly traced my steps backward until completely out of sight in the adjoining office. But, I could still hear them talking. I got up to leave.

"The trial is almost here, Breanna. How do you feel?" Tyler asked Breanna. I stopped, sat back down, and searched my handbag for my car keys.

"They still don't know what happened," Breanna answered.

"No?" Tyler asked.

"Not really." She paused. "I was all over him, *ya' know.*"

"Is that how he fell?"

"Oh boy. He fell, right!" she said emphasizing "right!" After a moment of silence, she went on to say, "I like the pictures on your wall, Dr. Tyler. It reminds me of Bermuda; of me and Sean. That's the same picture you had on the wall at the hospital when I took my clothes off that day."

She was a piece of work.

"How do you feel now, Breanna?" Tyler asked.

"Don't worry, I am not going to take off my clothes."

I got up to leave, but my left leg had fallen asleep. I stood up and clinched my fists until the tingling subsided when Tyler asked, "You said that you were all over Sean."

"Do you know what I mean?"

"I think so."

"You see, Dr. Tyler, I could not let him get away with kicking me to the curb. Was I not good enough?"

I didn't understand what I was overhearing and apparently neither did Tyler because he asked, "What exactly are you saying, Breanna?"

She raised her voice but did not lose her composure. "He was not going to screw me over and run back to Fay. What does he think I am?"

"Please go on, Breanna."

"Aren't I pretty enough? Wasn't I good enough?" She stopped and caught her breath.

"I'm so sorry, Dr. Tyler. I tried to tell him that we could work it out—that I wanted him in my life, that I didn't want to let him go."

Breanna's words were hitting very close to my heart. I had just told Craig some shit like that. We were on opposite sides of the law, yet our plight in some ways similar. Focus on Breanna. What happened to Sean was an accident—wasn't it? I tried to quiet the part of me that shared public opinion. I must believe in Breanna. Otherwise, the jury would see the doubt.

She continued, "I wanted him dead." Her voice was so low that I could not make out the rest of whatever she was saying.

She cried. She cried for her mother. She cried. I recalled the last time she told this story she freaked out at her home and tried to toss her body out of a closed window. "But, I didn't mean to hurt him," she recovered.

I jotted down a note to talk with Walter about not letting her testify. I couldn't take the chance; she was still too emotional. She couldn't even bring herself to look at photos of the scene. I got up to leave again. It would be unethical to stay any longer. My left leg was okay now.

I left a note for Tyler to call me on the front door.

On the way out, I saw James' car drive by. Great.

I tried to sneak out to avoid him. No such luck.

"Stop right there, you fine-looking *thang* you." James caught me just as I was putting the key in the door of my car. He hadn't seen me since I colored and cut my hair.

"James."

"When are you going to let me take you out, off the record?"

"I think we both agree that the most important thing right now is getting Breanna out of this trouble."

"I'm sure she'll be okay. Have you ever lost a case?"

"Yes, I have, James. This is very serious."

"She's in there now," he said, motioning back to Tyler's office. "What do you think of the shrink?"

"James, I need to catch Walter before he leaves for Bermuda."

"I thought you weren't leaving for another month."

"Walter wants to be there for the pre-trial hearing and some other outstanding discovery issues. The other side wanted us to produce her diaries but we've objected."

"When are you leaving?"

"Couple of weeks," I said and opened my car door

"Are you still going out with the TV guy?"

"Craig Nicks."

"Craig—what kind of name is Craig? I saw him the other night. I thought that was you with him, but it was someone else."

I couldn't give James the satisfaction of my curiosity so I said, "James, you are sick." I tried desperately to lighten the mood. "You had your chance."

"When are you going to give me another chance?"

"I don't do married men."

"But you had me first." I smiled at James and pulled out of the parking lot. Who the hell was Craig out with the other night?

When I got back to the office, Ola and my paralegal were in the lobby, instructing movers and shippers on the boxes and office equipment to be sent to Bermuda. We were setting up an office at the hotel over there.

"Walter said he'll call you tonight," Ola said.

"He's gone?" I asked.

"He just left. Also, a Dr. Lillian Schwid called. The number is on your chair."

"Who?"

"Dr. Schwid. No message, just a number." It could be one of the PMS doctors. I had placed a few calls, but we'd already decided to use Tyler as our expert to testify on how distraught Breanna was after the tragedy.

"Spiegel Cullen for a Dr. Schwid," I said into the phone.

She got on the line. "I'm your new doctor, Ms. Cullen. Dr. Oates has retired." She paused. "We have tried to reach you with the results of your physical."

Only then did I recall getting a letter or something in the mail about the new doctor. "Good for Dr. Oates," I joked.

"Ms. Cullen." Her voice was serious. "Your blood test is abnormal. We'd like you to see a specialist."

"Abnormal? Do you mean iron-poor blood?"

"Your white blood cell count is considerably high."

"The whites are a little high?" I repeated.

"They are considerably high, and we have an appointment scheduled for you this afternoon at three to see Dr. Steven Kline."

"This afternoon?"

"He's a good doctor. I know him personally."

"Specialist?"

"He is a hematologist."

"Okay. Thank you." I hung up and called Craig, but he was out of town. I didn't know he'd be away. I felt sad and lonely on the way to see this Dr. Kline. As I walked in the lobby of the hospital, I immediately felt ill. Hospitals made me sick. The guard at the podium in the lobby smiled as I walked by.

The elevators were slow as hell. What was wrong with me?

Hematologist? Is that a blood doctor? Blood? Blood doctor— couldn't be HIV—could it? I looked great. I was over the sore throat. I felt fine, other than being nervous about being in a hospital. I should sue that damned doctor, all of them old farts. Except Dr. Schwid, her voice was youthful. She seemed to be on the ball.

Finally, the elevator arrived, and I pushed with the rush of people to enter the small square of metal and wood to take me to the fifteenth floor. The elevator stopped at every other floor. My heart was racing and I was starting to hold my breath unwillingly. If the doors didn't open soon, I was going to pass the fuck out.

The door opened to an arrow pointing in the direction of "Hematology—Oncology." Oncology—isn't that cancer?

I wasn't going to make it. I thought of going back to the office. This was all an obvious mistake. Surely, I didn't belong there. I searched for understanding.

My legs wouldn't move. The elevator doors closed and I couldn't move. I rode to the thirty-fourth floor and then back down to the lobby. The arrow pointing to the telephones guided me. Hematology—that's blood, right? I didn't know *jack* about this medical stuff, but oncology meant cancer. I was scared.

Call mom. I tried to calm myself. My thoughts were random and quick. My mom was a seamstress. She was usually home during the day, especially during the winter months, busy making wedding-gowns for spring weddings. She even hand-beaded the dresses.

"Mom, what are you doing?"

"Watching *Divorce Court*. Would you shut up already?" she said, yelling at the TV. "Baby, I'm glad you didn't go into this stuff."

"Mom. . . "

"How are you, dear?"

"Mom, the doctor said my blood test is abnormal. She wants me to see a hematologist."

"Oh no, honey. You need a shrink, not divorce court," she continued talking to the television screen. "What are you saying, baby?"

"I'm at the hospital right now, but the sign said hematology—oncology."

I had her attention now. "You are at the hospital? What hospital? I'll be right there."

"No, I'm going back to the office."

"What did they say?"

"I didn't go. There must be some sort of mistake." Were they even checking for iron-poor blood like they were supposed to do?

"Spiegel, you are at the hospital—go see the doctor. I'll pray to St. Theresa."

"You think that I should go back up?"

"Yes, yes! I'll get dressed. Call me back as soon as you have seen the doctor. I'll pray."

I went back. The elevator came right away this time. I pressed the button again for the fifteenth floor. The nurse took me back right away and pricked my vein. I watched as rich, dark red filled no less that ten five-inch clear tubes with colorful rubber caps.

"Why so much blood? Am I going to faint?"

"You should be fine."

Dr. Kline came out to greet me himself. Tall and thin, in his sixties, he had very thick salt-and-pepper hair and a very deep voice. "How are you feeling?"

"Good." We moved to a small examining room where he asked me to sit on the edge of a narrow hospital bed with a sheet of white paper covering the plastic surface.

"Fever, night sweats, appetite?" he asked.

"No. No. Yes, appetite always good. Are you a hematologist?"

"Yes. Hematologist, Oncologist—usually one and the same." He felt the side of my throat and underneath my arms before asking me to lie back on the table.

"Really." I braced myself. He massaged the side of my stomach and groin area. "What do I have?"

"Maybe nothing," he said, looking over my charts. "I'd like to test you for a virus and have you come back in a few weeks."

"I'll be on trial in a few weeks." That didn't seem to impress him.

"You are a lawyer?"

"Yes."

"It could be one of three things. It could be a cold, which may cause your white blood cells to be a little high. It could be mononucleosis. Are you familiar with that?"

"The kissing disease."

"Or, it could be leukemia."

"Leukemia. Well, I know it's not that."

"In any event, we need to run more blood tests and have you come back in a month or so."

"A month or a week?"

"I think a month would be fine. If you need to come in sooner, just call my office."

As soon as I got out of the building, I called my mom back. The line was busy and bounced to voicemail. I left a message that the doctor took blood and said that I was free to go.

Instead of going back to the office, I walked to the library, a block from the hospital. I found the medical section and looked up what I could on hematology and oncology. I double backed to the reference desk.

"Do you mean blood cancer?" the reference clerk asked.

"Never mind. Thanks." I practically knocked over someone as I left the library in such a hurry.

I headed back to the office. I thought better of calling a friend of mine who was a nurse. No, I'd better not; she might think that something was wrong with me. I'd call the Center for Disease Control. Disease? Oh, shit. What was going on? My head was spinning and I felt faint.

I steadied myself on a bench across the street from the library in Logan Square. The homeless convened all around me. The scents of musk and urine hung in the air. I unconsciously started to scribble the names of all the guys I'd slept with in the last seven years. As I recalled, all of them had had a look of perfect health.

The cell phone rang. "Spiegel. It's Aliá."

"No kidding."

"What's going on? Mommy and Dad are upset. They said you had to see a cancer doctor. Spiegel?"

"I just got out. I'd never been more scared."

"Are you going home now?"

"No. I'm going back to work."

"Well, you sound fine."

"I'm fine, Aliá. The doctor said it may be mono or a virus or something and that my white cells were high but should go down in a month or so."

"Are you still going to Bermuda?"

"Of course I am! Ola started moving the office out there today. I'm fine."

"Really?" she asked.

"Really."

"Good. Let me tell you about Ahmir." Typical, with Aliá, everything ends up being about Aliá. I love her.

"Ahmir?"

"Girl. I think he wants to get married. What time are you getting off today?"

"Late."

"I tell you what, we'll pick you up for dinner!" Once her mind was set there was no stopping her. "Tootsie's just opened on South Street. *Ahh, ahh!* Corn bread, fish, so good, peach cobbler, and real potatoes, girl!"

"Real potatoes?"

"Yeah girl, you know, not that boxed stuff. Potatoes like Mommy's—"

"I don't know how you stay so skinny as much as you eat."

"We'll pick you up around eight."

"Okay."

"Call Mommy and Dad," she said before hanging up.

I couldn't call them, they would ask way too many questions. It was probably nothing. I sat on the bench until traffic along the circle picked up, rush hour already. The stream of taxis and cars switched lanes, maneuvering toward the highways out of center city. I collected my thoughts and walked back to the office. I called Craig on the way, to no avail.

Chapter Sixteen

The biggest case since *Simpson*, I was pumped and ready for the spotlight, feeling better than ever, when the time came to leave for Bermuda. Even Craig was going to take off to be with me the first week of trial. But it was Felix who knocked on my door around midnight a week before we were set to go.

"What are you doing here at my house so late?"

He pointed to me and then to him. "This meeting never took place." He looked so much like James, standing there decked out in black.

"I thought you were in Bermuda. What do you want?"

He pushed past me. The cold air came with him.

"Come in?" I slammed the door.

"Is my daughter going to walk on this?"

"Felix, damn it, you know that this is a tough case."

"Are you going to be able to?" He paused. "I don't give a crapshoot about some image of justice. Did you get things squared away with your law license there?"

"You know that I'm set to go! You didn't come knocking on my door at this hour to ask me if I have my license to practice law in Bermuda."

"Are you aware that Dirk is on my payroll?" We stood facing each other. His breath was warm.

"What are you talking about?" I tugged at my long purple terrycloth robe.

"Quid pro quo." He blinked. "Our case is assigned to this Appleby Supreme Court Justice."

"Yes, what are you getting at?"

"Dirk was doing some investigation work for me. It appears this Justice Appleby has had some trouble with the law in California." He stiffened his back and stared me down. "His son has a traffic violation."

"Who doesn't have a traffic violation in California?" I shrugged and walked over to the sofa. "Is that why the trial was postponed to April?" I hesitated. "Felix?"

He followed me to the sofa but did not sit down. He stood over me. "I hold the deciding vote."

"Is this about the real estate?"

"I lost my wife. I am not going to lose my daughter."

"Have you spoken to Walter?"

"Walter knows the fucking deal!" He raised his voice. "Bermuda cannot afford to jeopardize tourism."

"What is going on?" Aliá yelled as she came downstairs.

"I thought you were alone."

"Is everything all right with Brea?" Aliá had slipped her blouse and jeans back on, but her hair was still wrapped in a beige silk scarf.

Felix walked out and slammed the door.

I looked at Aliá and shook my head.

"What the freak is his problem? I don't care who he is. What did he want?"

"Everyone is edgy. It gets that way before trial," I said.

"Do you think she'll beat this?"

"Do you think she should?"

"What is that suppose to mean, Spiegel?"

I flipped the lights off and turned toward the stairs.

Aliá stood in my way. "I know you don't think Brea did this on purpose." Her hands firmly affixed to her hips she demanded, "Do you?"

"I'm not going to get into this with you."

"Why not!"

I pushed her out of the way.

She followed close behind me and flipped my light on after I flipped it off.

"Get out of my face, Liá."

"Brea couldn't kill anyone. What are you thinking?"

"Get out of my face, Aliá," I said louder this time.

"Are you feeling okay, Spiegel?"

"I'll be fine if you get the hell out of here and let me get some sleep."

Aliá flopped on my bed and stretched out on top of the covers.

"What about the blood thing?"

Right back at her, "What about the blood thing?" I'd gone back but the tests were uncertain. I got into bed. "Why don't you get the hell out of my room and let me get some sleep."

The phone rang.

"Don't answer it!" I yelled.

"It could be Mommy." She rolled her eyes at me. "Hello." She answered and held the phone toward me. "Spiegel."

I didn't move.

She grinned and whispered, "It's Dr. Tyler."

"Tyler?" Okay, a calm voice in a raging sea.

Chapter Seventeen

As we entered the courtroom, television cameras captured the arrival of our first day of trial. The courtroom was a relic. The wooden pews were old. The wooden floor creaked with each step. Usually, a defendant sat in a glass box in the middle of the courtroom with armed guards if he or she was incarcerated. Breanna, however, sat next to me at counsel table. The scent of vomit lingered in the air around her. She had been in the bathroom all night long, with stuff coming out of both ends.

The Honorable Lordship Brian Appleby entered from a side panel wearing a long black robe and a powdered wig. A court clerk walked a few steps ahead of Lordship Appleby and asked us to rise.

Appleby took his seat at the dais, and greeted those assembled with a warm hello. "As most of you know," he said, "and for those of you who do not know, I like to think that trials in my courtroom will be short and free of drama. I am not so hopeful in this case, however, as I see half of you already assembled are members of the press." Light chuckles filled the room.

Aliá, sitting next to Tyler, winked at me. She looked especially pretty in a pink linen pants suit. I was proud to see her. Tyler nodded and I tried not to blush. He was wearing a black suit, white shirt, and a black bow tie. The ladies on both sides of the courtroom stole looks at him. His rich, brown, smooth skin brightened when he flashed a smile. Noticeably absent was Craig.

I had dressed hurriedly that day in a sharp navy blue suit, navy sheer stockings, and navy pumps. My white starched blouse was buttoned wrong but it was discovered too late to correct. I could feel my heart beating fast.

Kevin Perry was already at the prosecution table. Next to him sat Ann Fox, a slightly older assistant prosecutor, tall and comfortable in her voluptuous frame, wearing a black suit jacket and a floral print skirt. The empty jury box was off to the right of the courtroom.

The families of both the defendant and the deceased were out in great force. Even Charli was present, and looking very pregnant.

Appleby was hard on the press. "Under no circumstances will I tolerate a media playground. By that, I mean your role will be to observe. You are not participants. If one of you makes a wrong move, all of you will be banned from the courtroom. Do I make myself clear?"

A unanimous "Yes, Your Honor," resonated in the courtroom. Many of the journalists assembled were from the United States.

Appleby turned to address the lawyers next. "I understand that we are ready to begin the jury session. Am I correct?"

"Yes, Your Lordship," Walter said, also seated with me at counsel table. Stephen was at the table too.

"No, Your Lordship." Perry stood up. "We are prepared to file an application for an all-male jury." He gave papers to Appleby and then to Walter.

Stephen stood up ready to object but Appleby waved him to silence. "What grounds do you have to file such a paper?" Appleby asked. A hint of amusement echoed in his voice.

Perry spoke, "According to the Criminal Code Act of 1907, Your Lordship, when matters of an indecent nature are likely to arise, on application, we can ask the court for an all-male jury."

Stephen continued standing.

"What matters of an indecent nature?"

"Your Lordship. The body of Sean Thomas was photographed in the state it was found."

"Go on."

"Your Lordship. We believe it to be disrespectful to show the photographs of the deceased because they show his private area." He paused. "In some photos, Your Lordship, his penis looks to be erect."

Breanna gasped. Her cry distracted the proceedings but not Appleby. He flipped through the papers. "Motion denied."

Perry continued, "Your Lordship, we strongly disagree respectfully."

"And I strongly deny your motion," he snapped. "I think the panel can ascertain the appropriate facts from the evidence presented."

Perry sat down. Stephen sat down too.

"Very well," Appleby said.

He then ordered the court clerk, dressed in Bermuda shorts and a white shirt with a gold badge, to lead a panel of thirty-six Bermudians into the courtroom. From the thirty-six, our challenge was to get to twelve. Not too difficult a process since the twelve names were drawn at random, unlike in Philly where we get to pick. Reading the wide-eyed curiosity on their faces was easy as they walked into the room and sat. They surely did not look like the hanging-jury types. My job was to show reasonable doubt in the prosecutor's case asserting that Breanna was so upset with Sean that she killed him.

No *voir dire* in Bermuda, but Appleby as the lordship got to ask a few questions to discover any indifference for the Crown or the accused. "How many of you have read something about this case in the newspapers or seen something about it on TV?"

All but one person raised their hands.

"Sir, where do you live?"

They all laughed as the elderly gentleman struggled to explain that he did not watch television or read newspapers.

"Very well," Appleby said and went on to explain the case and the seriousness of their role as jurors. Bermuda being such a small island, three of the people on the panel were related to Perry or Appleby. They had to stand down immediately.

Other challenges prevailed, but the process did not take very long at all. By the time the approved list and the stand-by list had been prepared, our stomachs were growling for lunch.

Appleby adjourned. A few people in the gallery left the courtroom quickly. A tall dark-skinned gentleman sitting in the back of the courtroom caught my eye as he moved to the center aisle, joining the people leaving the courtroom.

He wore black shades in a courtroom where there was no sun. He stood out as he turned to face me and locked me in an uncomfortable stare. He didn't appear to be with anyone in particular, but he looked unbelievably familiar. I asked Stephen if he'd recognized the guy, but as I turned to point him out, he fled the courtroom.

By around four-thirty both sides had agreed on a jury. The jury consisted of fourteen people, including two alternates. Eight women and six men; both alternates were women. One could never tell with a jury. We left the courtroom scheduled to come back the day after next.

Tyler, who had family on the island, had offered to drive Aliá and me back to the hotel. While we waited for him on the courtyard steps, Aliá said, "I like Dr. Tyler. Spiegel, what about you?"

"He's short," I said. I never considered him romantically, never allowed myself to see beyond that damn James, I meant Craig. "He's smart, though."

"That's not even what I meant and you know it."

"Tyler is not my type."

"He looks at you like you are sure his type."

"He has an ex-wife."

"And?" She twisted her mouth to one side. "He likes you, Spiegel."

"Oh, I don't know. I think that he is just one of those guys that likes people."

We walked out toward the street and waited for Tyler to pull up. He drove a chocolate Benz, customized. Tyler's father worked for years on the Bermuda Railway and managed to save a bundle of money. When he died, Tyler and his mother became very wealthy. The car had belonged to his father. Aliá and I both smiled when we saw him coming. We lost the smiles when we saw Charli in the front seat.

"What is she doing?" I hated James in that moment.

"I don't know but we are about to have some fun," Aliá said.

I was in no mood to play frick and frack with Aliá. "What is she doing in the car?" Aliá was beaming mischievously.

Tyler cocked his head. "Is there a problem, Aliá? Spiegel? James asked me to escort his wife to the restaurant, since their car was full."

"Restaurant?" I asked.

"Yes. He said we're all to meet there for dinner. Your partner and the others have left already."

"Hi," I said, as I opened the passenger-side front seat and asked Charli if she wouldn't mind getting in the back seat. "I have a few things I want to discuss with Tyler; would you mind very much, Charli, sitting in the back seat?"

"My goodness, no—not at all. Just give me a few minutes to get out. I move twice as slow now that I am pregnant."

"How pregnant are you?" Aliá asked once we were all seated in the car.

"Jeez. I'm seven months. Twins!"

"Twins!" Aliá echoed her excitement while I stewed.

"Boys? Girls? What?"

"James wants to be surprised."

With each answer I felt a jab in my heart. I wished Aliá would shut up but she was on a roll. "How long have you known James?"

"We actually grew up in the same neighborhood. I moved away. I ran into him quite by chance at a political event and well I guess you can see the rest." She smiled as she pointed to her stomach. "I came to visit him one weekend and one thing led to another."

Yada. Yada. Yada. I wanted desperately to change the subject but couldn't think of anything to say. Maybe I'd tell her that I had her husband first. I just wanted her fat ass out of the car. When I finally lifted my face, Tyler was eyeing me suspiciously, almost understandingly. I looked in his direction and his flirtatious smile brightened the mood.

"Are you teed about something?" he whispered as he pulled up to the curb outside a place called the Pickled Onion.

Teed? Who uses that word? I smiled.

He said louder this time, "Would you ladies like to get out of the car here and I'll find a parking spot?"

The restaurant was located on Front Street. Two-story outdoor restaurants, shops, and pubs decorated one side of the street and the ferries docked in the harbor on the other side. Evidence of British culture could be found at any turn, but Bermuda seemed more today a blend of London and Beverly Hills. Charli, Aliá, and I walked up a flight of stairs into the main area of the restaurant. A richly tanned middle-aged bald guy was playing the drums softly and working some sort of sound system to a nice calypso medley of *Lady in Red*. Locals and tourist alike laughed and downed beers at the bar.

Walter and the others were already seated when we walked over to join them, by now a party of thirteen with Stephen's wife and their two tots.

Breanna sat quietly next to her father. He drank water now. The conversation at the table was pretty general. Stephen was going on and on about the history of the archipelago, some fancy name for Bermuda. Tyler held chairs for Aliá and Charli before he sat down. James was not at the table.

On the way to the ladies room, I bumped into him standing at the pay telephones in a hallway leading to the restrooms. "I didn't know that your wife was pregnant again."

He tossed his hands in the air and smiled, but only said, "She didn't wait too long, did she?"

"Congratulations."

He placed one hand in his pocket and scratched the top of his head with the other. He scratched his head for at least a minute. Fool. "There's more to it than you realize," he said.

"I'm sure." I tried to step around him.

He stepped closer to me and grabbed me with both hands. "Look at me, Spiegel."

I tried to wiggle from his grip, afraid he'd see more in my eyes then I wanted to reveal. I felt like a cat had crawled up in my belly and was trying to claw its way out. I was starting to perspire. How could I want and despise him at the same time?

He pushed me against the wall and placed both hands underneath my skirt. "No underwear! Damn! You turn me the fuck on!"

I pushed him away. "Get your crazy ass away from me." If I didn't get back to the others Aliá or worse Tyler would come looking for me.

"I need you, Spiegel."

"And, what would you need her for exactly?" Charli stood at the doorway.

I walked away.

Chapter Eighteen

As forecasted, Friday morning was warm and bright as we gathered for the second day in the Supreme Court of Bermuda for the case against Breanna Jordan. "All Rise!" announced the court clerk. Everyone, packed into the only courtroom on the island that was wired for cameras, stood in place.

The spectators filled the rows in the back. I took a deep breath and blew it back out slowly, quietly. The sunlight streaming through two huge windows that stretched from floor to ceiling seemed to energize the people in the room. Breanna's entire family sat in the battered wood pews directly behind us while the family of the late Sean Thomas sat on the opposite side, watching Breanna intently and whispering to one another.

Everyone hushed and stood as Lordship Appleby swiftly entered the room and ascended the dais.

"Court is now in session," bellowed the court crier.

"Good morning," Lordship Appleby said, and briefly waved a hand. "I understand from both sides that we are now ready to begin." He glanced over at the court clerk and asked for the jury, then scanned the counsel tables and settled into his chair. The jurors entered in single-file from a side door. As they moved swiftly past the counsel tables to the jury box, some stared straight ahead while others walked with their heads down, avoiding eye contact until they were seated.

Then Appleby gave us an overview of what to expect, beginning with Act One—the opening statements–where the stage is set. "The barristers for both parties will tell you what they believe happened that resulted in your being here today," he explained. "They each will call witnesses to support their sides of the story." He removed a white hankie from his robe and blew his bulbous nose before ending a two-minute spin on what lawyers technically refer to as the direct examination of a witness, the re-direct, the cross, and the re-cross. "Lastly," he continued, while shifting in his seat to return the hankie to his pocket, "after you have been presented with all of the evidence, the barristers will conclude with their closing arguments." He briefly explained the grand finale and then turned his attention to the prosecutor.

Kevin Perry took his first shot. In sixteen years of practicing law, he had never lost a case. Comfortable in the courtroom, Perry stood and faced the jury. Clean-shaven, he looked exceptionally polished in his dark, well-tailored suit. As he neared the jury box, I wondered if he was going to look for the eye of the defendant and extend the customary accusatory finger.

"My name is Kevin Perry," he began. "I am the director of public prosecution for the Commonwealth of Bermuda. The evidence in this case will show, ladies and gentlemen of the jury . . . " Mrs. Wiggins, a fat, big-haired juror, dropped a pencil and bent over to find it. "The evidence will show," Perry repeated, "ladies and gentlemen of the jury, that the defendant in this case, Breanna Jordan, on May 7, 1999 was a twenty-four-year-old college graduate."

He paused, and then continued, "The evidence will show that on that same date Sean Thomas was thirty years old and engaged to a woman by the name of Fay Summer, who resides in Philadelphia, Pennsylvania. Sean was the parking attendant at a five-star Philadelphia hotel." Perry walked to the jury box and stood facing them.

"The evidence will show further that, on that date, at approximately one o'clock in the morning, the defendant," and here he turned and pointed a judgmental finger at Breanna—who sat frozen in her seat—"the defendant, Breanna Jordan, rammed her scooter, maliciously, intentionally, into Sean, causing him to fall to his death from the cliff of Horseshoe Bay on Route 13 here in Hamilton Parish on the island of Bermuda." He lowered his index finger and turned again to the jurors. "The charge in this case is murder. Was this an accident? No! Absolutely not! You will hear testimony that the defendant boarded a plane back to Philadelphia without informing anyone of the incident, except for a telephone call to her father, a United States *congressman*."

I tensed up. Earlier, both the defense and prosecution mutually had agreed not to drag the congressman into this trial any more than absolutely necessary.

"You will hear that the defendant did not return immediately for questioning; that it was not until a warrant was issued for her arrest that she returned to plead not guilty."

Perry went on for what seemed like hours about the evidence to be presented before he reached for the psychological anchor —the victim. He took a moment to survey the jury and shook his head.

"The defendant said that she was scared, that it was an accident. On the contrary—she felt betrayed and rejected. Sean was breaking up with her, and that was the last straw. She claims that Sean fought with her and that she struggled to get away. Ladies and gentlemen, the evidence in this case tells a completely different story." With that line, Perry wrapped up his opening argument and took his seat.

The courtroom was still when Appleby's secretary, a tall thin man, abruptly entered the courtroom from a side door. The secretary handed Appleby a note, and then stood by, waiting for a response while Appleby read, his eyes widening. We studied him—he'd become lost in the note. The courtroom was quiet; we were waiting to be dismissed for lunch.

Instead, Appleby adjourned for the day. It was a highly biased move. "It is already one o'clock and if the defense's opening takes, as expected, the same length of time as the prosecution, it would be well past four o'clock at the end of the day." Walter was right. The courts on the island were a little more relaxed than in the States. Appleby took frequent breaks and closed each day at four. "Court will reconvene Monday morning, nine o'clock." He stood quickly.

Now the jury would have the weekend to digest Perry's words without the benefit of mine. "Your Lordship!" I said. "Could we stay a few minutes longer to complete the opening defense?"

He just waved his hand. His decision was final.

"Your Lordship?" Again, he ignored me.

"The jury is dismissed until Monday morning." I'd have to wait.

After watching the others pile into cars waiting to take us back to the hotel, I jay-walked across the street and flopped on a bench overlooking the vast blue body of Hamilton Harbor. The Catalina Ferry, bobbing on the glistering waters, had just pulled into the crowded harbor and people wiggled to keep their balance as they stepped onto the platform. I thought of Perry's words. "Ladies and gentlemen," I mimicked Perry, "the evidence tells a completely different story." His words ricocheted through my brain. I kicked off my pumps and thought back to almost a year ago, to the day that this story began.

I sat on that bench for hours, staring out at the rippling blue waters. At that rainy Mother's Day race, when James tracked me down to take on Breanna's case, all I could think of was how much I loved James and how bad I felt about Breanna. Of what happened to Sean. Tears started to well up in my eyes as a stranger peering at me from a distance came into focus.

I wedged my feet back into my pumps and walked to the corner to hail a taxi back to the hotel. I called my mother—I wanted to hear her voice. As expected, she made me laugh describing her adventures at the mall with my dad. I hung up smiling. Then I called Craig. No answer. My smile disappeared.

The weekend passed quickly. We got a call on Sunday night that the lordship wanted counsel to report to his chambers the next morning at eight o'clock sharp.

When we arrived, Perry, his team, and a juror, Rose Wiggins, already had gathered in the small chambers behind the courtroom. Lordship Appleby was dressed in a white shirt and black Bermuda shorts. His black judicial robe hung on a cast-iron coat rack near his door. A built-in bookcase decorated one wall. Piles of legal papers lay all over his mahogany desk. His secretary brought in additional chairs so that everyone could be seated.

A court reporter was also present. Usually if a judge called one into chambers, it was serious.

"On Friday," Appleby began, "I received a note from my secretary that juror number six had an emergency she needed to discuss, and she could only discuss it with me. Sensing the urgency of such an unusual request, I met with Mrs. Wiggins, which is what precipitated the events this morning."

Appleby's secretary picked up a stack of papers and began handing them out to the lawyers. "I have prepared for each of you a copy of her statement."

Mrs. Wiggins, a widow, lived alone in a condo on a small beach resort. She sat with her head upright but her eyes shifted toward the floor.

I read through the statement while Appleby continued, "Essentially, someone called the home of Mrs. Wiggins and said, 'I'm watching you,' threatening to and I quote 'get her if she did not send Breanna to jail.'" Mrs. Wiggins' gaze shifted to Appleby while he continued to read. I was aghast.

"She states further," he continued, "that she did not recognize the voice but that it was a female. She has not discussed this matter with anyone but after the calls did not stop, felt it necessary to contact me."

Mrs. Wiggins glanced toward me. She did not speak. She blinked and turned again to Appleby. Appleby put the statement down on his desk. "For the protection of the juror, the record of this proceeding will be sealed."

When questioned by Appleby, Mrs. Wiggins sat up and said that she could and wanted to continue.

"Very well," Appleby said. His tone was compassionate. There were no objections. "So ruled."

Appleby looked at Mrs. Wiggins and said, "It is further ruled that the jury will be sequestered for the two-week anticipated duration of the trial. Said location of the jurors will not be disclosed."

"Excuse me, Your Lordship?" Mrs. Wiggins brought his attention back to her. "What do you mean by sequestered?"

"It means you will be given ample time this afternoon to collect your personal belongings from home and a police officer will escort you to a hotel for the duration of the trial for your safety in this matter."

"Just me?" she asked.

"All of the jurors," Lordship Appleby said. "It was one of the items explained to you earlier that could happen although it was not likely. It has now become necessary." He walked over to the coat rack and put on his robe. "Are there any further questions?"

"No," she said and tapped the side of her face with her index finger.

"We are done here." In walked a court clerk to escort Mrs. Wiggins to the jury room. "We will also have a police officer with the jurors at all times," Appleby said, off the record. "The telephone records will be subpoenaed and handed over to the police for investigation."

Mrs. Wiggins exhaled loudly enough for everyone to hear.

We left Lordship Appleby's chambers and took our places at counsel table. Appleby and the jury entered a short time later. As ordered, two armed police officers sat solidly near the front row near the jury box.

"Ms. Cullen?" Appleby said once he was seated at his dais.

I willed myself to stand up and move toward the jury. Breathe! Ready! Set! I tried to chill the nervous voices inside my head. Walter and I were each responsible for different parts of the trial. I was up for the opening statement. Go!

"Ladies and gentlemen," I began, "my name is Spiegel Cullen, as you know. I represent Breanna Jordan, who is the defendant in this trial." I walked over and stood next to her. I contemplated touching her face lightly, thinking that that might offset Perry's judgmental finger pointing on Friday.

"Now, you've had the weekend to think about what Mr. Perry told you on Friday. He forgot to tell you, however, that he has the burden of proving the case against Bermuda—I'm sorry, Breanna Jordan. And, indeed he has a heavy burden, because the evidence will not support that a murder was committed; there simply was no intent here. This was nothing more than a *tragic accident; an accident.*" Repetition was the number-one element of persuasive arguments. "The evidence will show a relationship filled with lies, manipulation, and yes love, but not murder."

"Look." I slowly walked from one side of the jury box to the other, making a point to connect with each one of them. "Here is what the evidence will really show. Breanna has had to handle a lot in her young life—losing a mother at a young age.

"You will find out that she made one telephone call from Bermuda to her father, because she was scared. She knew that Sean did not return to the hotel room, but she did not know why. You will hear from a psychologist that when Breanna learned that Sean was in fact dead, that he had drowned in the waters of Bermuda, she became hysterical.

"So, as we begin to put the pieces of this relationship together, I would ask that you as a jury look very carefully at the character of my client, Breanna Jordan, and that of Sean Thomas. I will travel right along with you, day after day, until the puzzle is complete. You can count on me to give you the best possible picture of what really happened. There are no winners here. A life is gone and another life is ruined. What really happened?" I opened my hands. "The police, in their rush to judgment, looked no further than Breanna. But my client is innocent."

I glanced at the alert jury on the way back to the counsel table. Right now, they were the most important people in the world. Mrs. Wiggins looked at me without blinking. "Yes," I told them, "Breanna quarreled with Sean, but she did not kill him." I took a moment to study the bright focused eyes of each juror. "She did not kill him." And, that was *that*.

Chapter Nineteen

On the third day of trial, the man who removed Sean's body from the water, Chief Coroner Henry Orr, was the first witness to place his hand on a Bible and promise to tell the truth.

Perry grilled him. "Excuse me, Mr. Orr, are you saying that Sean Thomas could not have hit his head during his fall from the cliff?"

"I am saying that a significant amount of blood was found on a rock embankment about a mile from the cliff."

"Now, Mr. Orr, let's be realistic. There was no one else present other than the victim and the defendant. Isn't it possible that Sean hit his head when he fell, then his body was swept a few miles ashore where he lay whacked and bloodied?"

"I guess it is possible, however—"

"Did you say it was possible?"

"Yes, but—"

"Thank you; asked and answered." Perry turned his back on Orr and strolled back to his table.

After lunch, Walter conducted the cross-examination, allowing Orr to complete the answer Perry had interrupted earlier.

"Would you say, Mr. Orr, that Sean Thomas may *not* have hit his head on a fall subsequently causing his death?" Walter asked.

"Yes."

"Would you elaborate?"

Orr tugged on the lapels of his suit jacket. "The body was found face down between several rocks. It is likely that the deceased suffered trauma to the head and fell forward."

"And do you think, as the prosecutor would have us believe, that Sean Thomas hit his head during a fall from the cliff?"

"Anything is possible." He hunched his broad shoulders. "It could have happened either way."

"Would you answer the question, please?"

"The rocks at the bottom of the cliff were a few feet from directly under the cliff. And—"

Walter interrupted. "He could not have fallen straight onto the rocks?"

"As I said, anything is possible. But—"

"I'm sorry, please continue."

"If the fall had caused such severe bleeding, the evidence of such would have been washed clean from the water, given the location."

"Thank you, Mr. Orr." Walter turned to Appleby. "No further questions."

"Re-direct?" Appleby asked Perry. Perry got another shot at Orr. "Can you please explain to the jury, Mr. Orr, the injuries sustained by Mr. Thomas according to your report?"

"May I have some water, please?" He wiped the sweat from his brow. The court clerk shuffled to get him water.

"The condition of the body, Mr. Orr," Perry prompted.

"Head trauma, a broken left leg, multiple lacerations to the face, and fluid in the lungs." Orr tugged again at his suit jacket.

Perry swirled quickly to face the witness. "Fluid—do you mean water?"

"Yes. He was alive when he hit the water, though. There was air and water in his lungs."

"Do you have an opinion as to what caused his death?"

"As it states in my report, the head trauma likely was caused by either the subject hitting a blunt item at a high rate of speed, or something hitting him."

"And the broken leg?"

"The injuries are consistent with a fall."

"Now, Mr. Orr," Perry said. "How long would you estimate that the body of Mr. Sean Thomas was in the water?"

"I would say one to two days at the most. We had low tides, so the body stayed close to the shoreline. He could have washed out or been eaten by the sea life."

"Did you say eaten by sea life?" Perry knew damn well that was exactly what was said.

"Objection, Your Lordship. Cause for speculation," Walter shouted.

"Overruled."

Perry sat down. "Nothing further."

Walter stood yet again for more on the cross-examination.

"Mr. Orr," Walter said, flipping through the autopsy report. "Were there traces of alcohol or drugs found in Sean's system?"

"Yes, I did find traces, a low percentage of alcohol and a high chemical number for marijuana."

"Enough to render him intoxicated?"

"Yes." That answer planted in the minds of the jurors the idea that Sean may have fallen to his death by his own hand. He could, as Walter had always said, have tripped over his own fucking feet.

Lordship Appleby recessed around four o'clock.

As we prepared to leave the courtroom, I thought of how the jury needed to hear in Breanna's own words that Sean's death was an accident, that she had left him alive, or so she thought. But, she was fragile, like a dinner mint on a hot day. She had been quietly sitting in the courtroom. The only time she cried was when she saw the photograph of Sean.

I forced myself to forget the conversation I'd overheard between Breanna and Tyler—that she wanted him dead. I scanned the crowd and made my way over to Breanna.

"Do you want to grab a bite to eat, just you and me?" I asked.

"Where are we going to be able to go, Spiegel, with all of these reporters?" Breanna said.

I had to get her ready to testify. "My room—room service," I said. She forced a smile and peered at me from behind dark glasses.

James was watching us and Charli was watching him. I had not seen much of James—and none of Craig—since the trial started. You'd think Craig would at least call to say, "I'm thinking about you, *dang.*" I looked forward to Mom and Aliá calls at the end of the day.

I rode to court that morning with Tyler and motioned for him to join me, as I slipped my arm around Breanna and prepared to tackle the press. James also hurried in our direction.

Breanna stiffened. She stopped and began to scream. She was flipping out again. And she had been doing so well.

"Ohmygod! Sean! Sean! I always knew you were alive. I *knew* it."

A man lunged toward her, his fist clenched tight.

"That's the guy!" I screamed.

James jumped between Breanna and the guy. Pure hatred filled his eyes as the guy fell hard, missing the punch he had intended for Breanna. James grabbed him by the back of his shirt and tossed him aside. Sheer pandemonium erupted in the wide aisle dividing the courtroom. The courtroom deputies tried to separate the two men. Sean's family surrounded the man who had thrown the punch. Some of the people were yelling. "Sam, stop it! Sam, stop it!"

The guy broke away from his pack and headed toward James. "You mo' fucker! She killed my brother!" He hit James with such force that it split his lip, and blood splattered in my direction. Breanna passed out and Felix grabbed her. I ran to James and fell on my knees in front of him while his wife ran to his side. Sam, now surrounded by guards, was being escorted out of the room in handcuffs.

Dirk jumped into the fray and took charge bellowing. "Clear the courtroom, please!" The security guards came from out of nowhere to assist. I thought for sure that Appleby would have peeked out from his quarters. His secretary appeared instead with a bag of ice and paper towels for James.

Tyler lifted me from my knees. "Let's get out of here."

"Let's get Breanna back to the hotel," I said.

"She will be fine," Tyler responded. "Who the hell . . .?"

"Sam Thomas," Dirk said and motioned behind him. "Sean's brother. Is that the guy you saw in the library?"

"Yes."

"And at the beach?"

"Yes," I said.

"I'll take care of him," Dirk said. "He just brought himself a jail cell. Are you okay?"

"I'm fine. How is Breanna?" She was sitting up now with her head in her hands.

"I never even knew that Sean had a brother," Breanna said.

Felix searched the room for anyone in authority willing to listen to him. "Ignorant. If the family cannot control themselves, they should not be allowed in the courtroom."

Appleby's secretary shook his head. Tyler nudged me. "Let me take you back to the hotel, Spiegel."

"I'm okay," I said noticing the sprinkling of James' blood on my blouse. "Is James alright?" I wiped my hand over the blood. I didn't think that would remove it, yet I just wanted to touch it.

"He left with his wife." Tyler pointed to the door. "I think he may need a few stitches."

"I guess we better get out of here as well." I hung my head. I was so transparent when it came to James.

"Are you okay?" Tyler lightly brushed my hair.

Instinctively, I faced him. He pulled his hand back quickly. "It's going to be a long night and yes, I'm okay." I had to review for tomorrow. Fay Summer was scheduled to take the stand.

Tyler watched me as he extended his arm to escort me out.

He took me back to the hotel and I went directly to my room to get comfortable. I wanted the trial to be over. I made a note to ask Dirk to get records from all chartered flights from Philly to Bermuda during the time of the incident. I had a strong hunch that maybe Sam had been on the island, but was grasping for something, anything. I wanted Breanna to come home. I wanted James to—to what?

"Just a second," I responded to the knuckles on the door. I peeked through the peephole.

"Are you fucking all right?" I asked James. I was "fucking" everything, fucking this, fucking that. I opened the door quickly.

He came in and stood behind the closed door. "You won't have to worry about that guy anymore."

"Are you pressing charges?"

"Hell, yeah!"

"How you feeling?" I asked and pulled the belt to my black satin robe tighter.

"I came to make sure that you were okay. Were you in the shower?" He walked to the edge of my bed, sat down, and grabbed the hotel magazine off the nightstand. "How about if we order room service?" Aside from the bruised lip, James looked good. He glowed with a reddish Indian hue. The island sun agreed with him.

"James, what are you doing here?" I was feeling *some kind of way.* "Stop fucking playing with me." I felt my hair loosen and slowly fall.

"I think I love you, Spiegel." I had assumed he did at one time—boy, was I wrong. "Can I kiss you?"

"James, what are you talking about?" With the looks of that lip, he wouldn't be kissing anyone for awhile.

"I think I've always loved you." Maybe they gave him more than stitches at that hospital. Perhaps, they gave him something that affected his brain. "I married the wrong girl."

"You have only been married a year," I said.

"Do you love me?" He stood up and pulled me to him. "I love you. No matter what happens, I am going to make things right between us."

I had him first, Mrs. Charli. "James," I whispered like we were in a crowded room, "it's too late." I should take him, though, one more time for old time sake.

James was not his usual arrogant crazy self. He was sincere. "If you love someone you should tell them . . . I know that now."

"We had our time, James. It's too late."

"You don't love me?" he snapped.

"James . . . you'd better go." I was no home wrecker after all.

"Why are you always throwing me out? I have so much I want to tell you. It is killing me, watching you every day, seeing the way that shrink looks at you. We should be together. Are you willing to throw ten years away?"

I backed away, but was still close enough to feel the heat coming from his body. "James, you threw us away."

His crazed glare pierced every part of me. "I'm sorry." He came closer. "Do you want me to beg?" He twirled in a circle. "Miss high and mighty! Is that what you want?"

"Get the fuck out of here, James." I didn't even recognize my own voice. "Get out, get out, please just go!"

Chapter Twenty

It took me awhile to settle myself after I threw James out last night. Denying him, however, made me want him more.

Appleby called a one-day recess after the commotion in the courtroom involving Sean's brother, so I decided to spend the day with Breanna. I thought we'd go for something to eat on the beach since the April weather was so unusually warm and sunny.

She was waiting in the lobby dressed in a zebra-print bathing suit and long black skirt, her eyes still hiding behind large-framed dark shades.

"Breanna," I told her, "you have to show some emotion." She seemed detached, as if the whole mess would somehow disappear.

"I don't think that I want to take the stand," she said.

"I think that the jury needs to hear from you." Needed to hear in her own words that she meant Sean no harm, that the whole thing was an accident.

"I'll never say that I killed Sean." We talked and walked outside to wait for the jitney to the beach.

"Good."

"And, I am not insane!"

"Of course not. But, you must understand that you are on trial here for your life."

"My life . . ."

"They can send you to jail."

"Jail? Where? Here?" Her bottom lip dropped to her chin. Her eyes widened. Was she finally hearing me?

"I don't want to upset you, Breanna." We stopped and stood at the gazebo near the hotel entrance. "You hit Sean, you hurt him, you may have even killed him." I was starting to visualize my closing argument. The visual was not good.

"I know enough from my law studies to know that it was not murder. It was an accident," she said weaving her neck side to side. Her hair had started to grow and she had pulled it back in a long, phony ponytail that moved with her bobbing head.

"Can you leave the shades at home?"

"I look horrible."

"You are *supposed* to look horrible. Let the jury see you. Let's go over your testimony."

"I totally freaked when I saw that guy yesterday. I didn't even know Sean had a brother."

"Apparently, Breanna, there were a lot of things about Sean that you did not know."

"What else?"

"The fiancée."

"He didn't love that—I told you about her. He left her standing at the altar." She put her hands on what used to be hips. "And what is with her wearing all that black like she's some widow. Puh-leez!" Her hands fell to her sides. "Anyway, Sean felt sorry for her. *Ya' know* the kind."

"The kind?"

"Yeah. The kind that won't let go; the kind that hangs on, even after you tell them you want out."

"Are you talking about you or Fay Summer?"

She rolled her eyes at me and turned to smile at a stranger walking by the hotel. "Anyway, I think that I'm falling *in love* with Dirk." She stopped. I thought I saw her eyes well up. "He is so supportive. He calls. He sends me gifts." She paused. "And, he's good—"

I pulled her over to a standing taxi, deciding to forgo the beach for now. "I have a better idea."

"Where are we going?"

"St. George." Her Majesty's Prison, but that part I didn't tell her. It was the only co-ed prison on the island.

"St. George?" Breanna slowed her step.

"Where to, pretty ladies?" asked the taxi driver.

"St. George." I said.

"Where in St. George?" The driver eased out onto the road.

"The woman's prison"

"Wait one freaking minute! I'm not—" Breanna interrupted. The cab driver screeched the breaks.

"We are just going to see it, that is all!" I said.

"I don't know if I even want to do *that*," Breanna said. But, she eventually relaxed and went along for the ride.

We sat on opposite sides on the backseat and stared out the windows at the steady traffic of small cars and mopeds zooming along against the backdrop of smooth deep blue waters.

"Your island is beautiful," Breanna said to the driver.

"First time on vacation here?

"No; yes—no, not really," she said.

"Well, welcome."

We arrived in St. George in about twenty-five minutes and I paid the fare from a stash of Bermuda coins I'd been accumulating while on the island. The town looked different from the other parts of the island, densely populated and quaint, like the 1800s.

We couldn't actually walk on the prison grounds, but found a spot overlooking a three-story facility where we were able to sit on the grass a few feet from a barbed-wire fence.

"Are we going inside?"

"No. I thought we needed a change of scenery." I wanted her to see what would become her home away from home if she didn't snap into reality.

"I'm scared, Spiegel."

"Do you have a temper, Breanna?"

"Yeah, ya' knows I have a temper."

"And Perry may push you to see you come undone."

"And?"

"And, if we put you on the witness stand you have to control your temper. If you lose it on the witness stand, then you might as well kiss your fucking ass good-bye. "

"Damn, Spiegel!" She jumped up, shocked. "My dad—"

"This is your life, your dad cannot help you on the witness stand and I am not going to lose this case."

"But, my dad—"

"Forget your dad, Breanna!" I yelled. "Is your temper bad enough to make you kill someone?"

"I didn't kill Sean." She sat next to me and stared at the mauve colored walls of the prison.

"Listen to the question. It is very important that you listen to the questions."

"Okay. No, my temper isn't that bad."

"What I am about to say is very important. If Perry asks you a question, listen very carefully. But, if I object, do not answer until Lordship Appleby has ruled on my objection. Do you understand?"

"I think so." She paused. "I love you, Spiegel."

"I love you too, Breanna, but this has nothing to do with love. We are trying to bring you home and that will hinge solely on what the jury thinks of you."

"Damn it." She clinched her right fist in her left hand. "I'm tired of everyone deciding for me. What if Sean didn't hit his head on the fall? Does that make sense to anyone but me?"

Almost a whole year had passed, and Breanna was sustained by a sense of innocent trust that her father would make the nightmare go away. Suddenly, she looked at me with wide-eyed amazement, like the light bulb clicked on for the very first time.

She spoke with surprising authority. "Maybe the taxi man saw something." She stiffened her posture and looked me in the eyes. "Come on, will you help me?"

I felt her energy and was charged by it. "Help you to do what? I'm trying as best I can to keep your crazy ass out of jail."

She cracked up. "Do you have the address of that taxi driver's wife?"

"It's 213 Hiding Place."

"Let's go!" She practically pulled me around the grounds, to hail a taxi. Her glasses fell off and she barely stopped long enough to pick them up. "Come on. Get in." She pushed me into the taxi.

When we told the taxi driver the address he asked, "Are you sure?"

"Yes, we're sure. Step on it, please," Breanna said.

"I will take you wherever you want to go but 213 Hiding Place is not in the safest neighborhood. Do you understand?"

"Will you wait for us?" I asked.

He chuckled and turned around in his seat. "How long are you going to be?"

"I don't know." Breanna was doing most of the talking.

"I will try to come back but no, I can't wait."

"Okay, thank you," Breanna said.

We pulled in on Hiding Street—in an area perhaps somewhere between a war zone and a neighborhood. Only three big limestone houses stood on the block. A rooster cackled next to a fluffy black cat, both co-existing in the front yard. The main door was open and the tattered screen was dirty and unlocked.

Breanna tilted her head down and glared at me from behind her shades. "Why are you just standing there? Are we going to ring the bell?" she asked.

I loosened the button on my blouse and swallowed. We stared hard. "You ring the bell."

"Me!" She muffled her scream. "Let's both go ring the bell."

We dodged the broken steps leading to the pastel colored two-story house and rang the bell.

"Maybe we should go, Spiegel. I think that this is a crack house."

"No." I was scared but we'd come too far now. Besides, there are no crack houses in Bermuda. "Why would you say that?"

"Spiegel, there is no answer—can we go now?" Breanna was frightened, too.

"Come on, let's just go in."

"Are you nuts? Isn't that trespassing?" She stopped. "You are supposed to be the lawyer."

"Well, let's ring the bell again." I lightly pressed at the door to open it wider. "If you were not my client, I'd be out of here right about now. Let's peek in, and we can leave if no one is home."

"How do we know someone is not waiting in there with a gun?"

"Can I help you ladies?" A perfectly round-figured lady opened the door and looked at us with one eye closed.

"Hi. Yes. We are looking for a Mrs. Porter," I said.

"Who?"

I looked at my note. "Mrs. Potter, I'm sorry."

Breanna held on to my arm.

"I am Mrs. Potter." The strands of her hair that were not held by a bun fell into her face. "Who are you?" She asked in a soft Bermudian accent.

We stood at the door. Breanna spoke. "I am Breanna Jordan and this is Spiegel Cullen. We would like to ask you some questions about your husband."

"Are you from the police?" She squinted.

"No Madam. I am an attorney and we think that your husband may have had information in connection with the case involving the murder of the American at the beach."

"Oh, yeah." She nodded knowingly. "My man's a good man, but he done gone home." She opened the door and we entered, then the three of us simultaneously sat down on a flowered sofa.

"Did he tell you anything at all about a couple on the beach?"

"No, sugar." She watched Breanna as Breanna rudely pulled out her cell phone and called Dirk. While she asked Dirk to pick us up, the three of us sat there awkwardly.

"Is that one of those mobile telephones?" She pointed and grinned.

"Like I was saying," I shifted in my seat. "If you think of anything at all, would you please call me?" I handed her a business card.

"Just one thing," she paused. "When you think they gonna return my husband's belongings?" She got up to walk us to the door. "I know Pete had photos of me and him and the kids and stuff he kept in the taxi. That taxi was his second home, just the roads unsafe sometimes if people drive too fast."

Maybe Dirk, who was at that moment ringing Mrs. Potter's bell, would know how to help her get her husband's stuff. I promised her that I would check and get back to her.

"Thank you now. Thank you for visiting me. Nice ladies, are you?"

The neighborhood spectators had grown. They watched as we greeted Dirk and jumped into his car.

Breanna's glimmer of strength faded slightly until she saw Dirk. He clearly made her smile.

Dirk spoke, "I don't think I wanna know, but what are you doing here?"

"It's a long story," Breanna said.

He looked at Breanna. "I wanted to let you know that the guy, Sam Thomas, has left the island. He was wanted in Pennsylvania on another charge. Ready, pretty ladies?"

"Yeah, we better get back." I leaned back against the seat and sighed deeply.

"Okay, pretty ladies. We should get back." Dirk started the car and drove off.

Breanna said softly, "I wish I could take everything back."

Dirk twisted his head to the left and said to Breanna, "I was hoping to take you to dine if you like."

"Dirk, please keep your eyes on the road," she said and accepted Dirk's invitation. He smiled as he pulled the car to the side of the road to take a call.

"Oh yes, Ms. Liá. Your sister is right here."

"The girl is too resourceful," I said, taking the cell from Dirk. "Aliá, what's up? How did you track me down?"

"Your damn phone is not on—again! So, I just started calling everyone you know over there. Did you get my e-mail?"

"No. I have not been on the computer lately."

"First, some doctor called and wants you to come in about a blood test." She paused. "I thought you said everything was okay."

"It is. I'm fine. Do you want me to call you back when I get back to the hotel?"

"No. Just tell me yes or no if you will be back this Saturday and I'll make the appointment for Monday or Tuesday."

"Okay, go ahead and make the appointment."

"And, check your e-mail tonight. I sent you a really long one about Ahmir. And, tell my girl I said I love her and to hang in there."

"Okay, I'll tell her," I said, looking up across the seat at Breanna. "Love you, Sis."

"Okay. Love you, too," she said. "Give me a call tonight if you can," she said just before hanging up, "And, please thank that fine ass Dirk for the use of his telephone."

"Your sister should be a detective," Dirk joked, as I handed him back his phone.

"Thanks, Dirk."

"Anytime, pretty lady. Oops. There I go again."

"It is what it is," said Breanna, temporarily moving her gaze from the window. "Do you think that I am pretty, Dirk?"

"Most definitely, Ms. Jordan, and we are going to help get you out of this fine mess."

What a head case!

"You are welcome to join us to dine, Ms. Spiegel."

"No, thank you." Fay Summer was on the stand tomorrow and I had to prepare exhibits for Walter, who was doing the cross-examination.

Chapter Twenty-One

"She is a crazy bitch," I overheard Fay say to Sean's elderly uncle, as we jammed into the elevator up to the courtroom. The same uncle that read the obituary at Sean's funeral held the elevator for me. I'd object for sure if she said anything like that on the witness stand. It was going to be a hectic day. I was running late and had jumped onto an elevator crowded with what seemed like Sean's entire family.

When the elevator doors opened to the floor, I was the first one off and walked straight ahead into the already packed courtroom. I took a seat next to Breanna. A few seconds later, Lordship Appleby and the jury entered and Fay Summer was called to the stand.

"Do you swear to the tell the truth, the whole truth, and nothing but the truth, so help you God?"

"I do," she said and was sworn in on direct. Sure enough, she was draped in black. Stylish though—high spiked pumps, black fishnet stockings, an A-line skirt, and a white fitted stretch blouse. She had the kind of shape that would make men bump into walls.

Perry questioned her. "Now, Ms. Summer, can you please state your name and tell us how you knew the deceased."

"Um . . . Fay," she said with a southern drawl. Her parents moved her to Philly from North Carolina almost fifteen years ago and she still spoke with a southern drawl. "Summar." She crossed her long healthy legs. "Sean was my fiancée."

I glanced at Breanna and her nostrils started to wiggle as Perry continued. "How long were you and Sean engaged?"

"We were engaged for a year, but we've dated since I was ten years old."

"Had you and Mr. Thomas set a wedding date?"

"Yes." She fixed her bulging cat-like eyes on Breanna.

"And what was that date?"

"I don't remember, but we *had* set it."

"Do you know the defendant?"

"Yes, I know her. She is crazy."

"Objection!" I was on my feet.

"Ms. Summer, please answer only the questions asked," Lordship Appleby warned and looked down his nose over his glasses at Fay.

She looked up at Appleby and then to Perry. "No problem."

"How did you come to know the defendant?"

"I've known of her before she killed Sean."

"Objection," I said.

"Sustained. The jury will ignore that remark," Lordship Appleby warned again.

"Last April, about a year ago, she came to our house."

"Your house and Sean's house?" Perry asked.

"Yes. First she started calling every hour on the hour, demanding to speak to Sean."

"Did she speak with him?"

"No. I hung up on her and unplugged the telephone."

"What happened next?"

"A few hours later she was banging on our door, yelling and screaming that she was pregnant and that she was going to abort the baby herself that night with a hanger if Sean did not come out and talk to her."

"And did they talk?"

"Hardly. Next thing I knew they were fighting like wildcats. She is crazy, I tell you."

"Objection, Your Lordship."

"Sustained."

"Was Breanna arrested?"

"No. They never arrested her because of her daddy and all."

"Objection," I interjected.

"Sustained."

"No one was arrested that time," she answered.

"There were other times?" Perry questioned. "What do you mean?"

"Too many to count. She was always going loony—excuse me—she'd get upset, in front of my door whenever Sean tried to explain to her that he did not love her, that he loved, and wanted to marry, *me*."

"Ms. Summer, where were you on the night of Sean's death?" Perry wanted to rule her out?

"Excuse me?" She twitched in her seat.

"If you could state your whereabouts?"

"I was at home."

"In Philadelphia?" Perry asked.

"Yes, that is my home," she smirked. "May I have some water, juice, or something?" A tall, thin police officer stationed at the jury box poured her a paper cup of water from the pitcher resting on a small table between the witness box and the jury.

I scribbled a note: Fay—Philadelphia.

Perry continued after she gulped the water down in one swoop. "Why do you think that Sean went to Bermuda with Breanna?"

Fay squished the paper cup and held it between her long fingernails. "She probably begged him. I had told him if he did not break it off with her for good that I was out of his life forever. I thought he had broken it off with her; apparently not."

Perry's direct examination was over. He sat down.

I approached Fay Summer cautiously. We had talked about not even cross-examining her, but we wanted to show the manipulative nature of the deceased.

"Ms. Summer, did you love the Sean?"

"Yes. I loved him."

"And you were aware that he was dating other women."

"Yes, but I didn't kill him." She clinched her fist.

"Thank you for that, Ms. Summer. No further questions."

Michael Tyler was next to take the stand. He walked slowly and deliberately to the front of the courtroom as if he was showing off his navy Armani suit and matching tie. His locks were pulled back in place as was his neatly trimmed mustache.

After the preliminary litany of Tyler's education and experience, and whether he'd testified in prior litigation, he was ready. He glanced quickly at me. Tyler was our expert witness, so we questioned him first.

"Dr. Tyler, you examined the defendant shortly after the death of Sean Thomas?" I asked.

"Yes," he answered loudly.

"How would you describe her?"

"She was suffering from severe post-traumatic stress." He unbuttoned his suit jacket.

"And, what exactly does that mean?"

"She had an emotional breakdown. She did not know that Sean had fallen from the cliff or died, and became hysterical upon hearing the news."

Perry decided not to make this case a battle of the shrinks because we were not asserting that Breanna was insane. He did, however, stand up to cross-examine Tyler.

"Can you tell us when you first met the defendant?" Perry asked.

"Professionally?"

"Yes."

"A few weeks after the incident, her father brought her to me on the advice of a family doctor." Good. He did not say personally, and Tyler did not give up any more information than was requested.

"Dr. Tyler, have you ever had an opportunity to treat Ms. Jordan during which she exhibited, how do I say, well, inappropriate behavior?" What was he getting at?

"She suffered an emotional breakdown." Tyler shifted in his seat.

"Would such an emotional breakdown, Dr. Tyler, cause her to expose her breast to you during an examination?"

Shit! "Objection." Where was Perry getting this information? "On what grounds?"

"Your Lordship, there is no evidence to substantiate this line of questioning," I said.

"Your Lordship, if you will allow me a little room here, I can establish the nature of Ms. Jordan's mental capacity for manipulating people."

"Overruled. I will allow it. You may answer, Dr. Tyler."

"Yes. A mental breakdown can cause one to behave inappropriately."

"Is it true that Breanna Jordan, while you were treating her, began to take her clothes off, and that you had to tell her repeatedly to dress?"

"Inappropriate—"

"Yes or no, Dr. Tyler! Yes or no!"

"Yes."

"Is it true that only when you brought in a female nurse, Ms. Jordan composed herself appropriately?"

"Your Lordship!" I yelled.

Tyler stopped speaking.

Perry walked over to his table and his assistant handed him a piece of paper. No way Perry could have obtained a copy of Tyler's medical notes yet the line of questioning had to be from Tyler's report. Oh, god! Sean's brother that day in the library!

My hands were clammy. It would prejudice us if he had the actual report and the jury got to hear how Breanna stripped for Tyler. Instead though, he moved on. "Nothing further, Your Lordship." He didn't have it.

The next day, Stefany Fattah's testimony was explosive.

"Why do you think that Breanna stayed in the relationship with Sean?" Perry asked Mrs. Fattah.

She had changed her hair from straight to curly and from black to light brown. She was still a cover girl, though, with big brown eyes. "She loved him," Stefany said, and loosely tossed her spiral curls out of her face.

"Breanna loved someone that was cheating on her; inconsiderate of her feelings; having affairs with other women?" I asked.

"She loved him and I don't think that she'd ever had sex like she had with Sean." How embarrassing. But, Stefany Fattah didn't look bothered at all. She glanced at Breanna. An uncomfortable chuckle circulated the room.

Fuming, I faced the witness and spoke slowly, "Is that to say that in *your* opinion, Breanna was just too naïve for the likes of *Sean Thomas?*"

"Objection!" Perry yelled. "Cause for speculation."

"Overruled," Appleby said. "You may answer."

"Most definitely." She wiped the smile from her cover girl face.

"Thank you, Ms. . . . No further questions." I searched for her name. It wasn't coming to me fast enough. Get a grip. "Mrs. Fattah. Thank you."

Lordship Appleby adjourned and we now had a few days off.

As we pulled up to the hotel, I saw Tyler getting into a taxi with his luggage. He stopped just before stepping into the taxi and waved. A pair of running sneakers hung from around his neck. I'd forgotten that he was a runner. He was dressed in an off-white khaki suit, brown loafers and no socks. His luggage was piled in the backseat of the taxi.

"Tyler, are you leaving now?"

"Yes. I still have a practice to run in Pennsylvania."

"I know." I curved my eyes to the ground.

"Should you need to reach me at any time, you have all of my numbers," he said. "Anytime for anything."

"Bye, Dr. Tyler," Breanna said, as she brushed past him on the way into the hotel. She had a *date* with Dirk.

I felt like my best friends were leaving the island. One by one, like survivors, they were leaving.

We looked at each other for an empty moment.

He spoke first. "I would like to see you when you return."

"I would like that very much." I waved goodbye, gave him a hug, and went inside. He smelled good.

I stopped at the front desk to pick up my laundry and the clerk gave me a message—James wanted to see me that evening at nine. "My place or yours," the note read.

I also had a message from Craig on the voicemail.

"Hello, baby. I miss you. I hope you are having fun. My birthday is Friday and some friends are having a small party for me. I may not be around when you return. I'll catch up with you on Saturday."

"I've been away for at least ten days! His birthday is this weekend and he's talking about catching up with me when?" I yelled into the telephone. I dialed his number.

"Craig? Let me get this straight. You are having a party this weekend?"

"Oh, yeah."

"Craig," I said and was about to say something else before he cut me off, but my mind kept on churning. I let my screwed-up vision of what I wanted from Craig silence me. I hated putting up with his jog down the middle of the road and his take-it or leave it attitude.

He sounded nervous. "Before you say anything, Spiegel, I thought that you would have a lot of things to catch up on just getting back to town."

I don't know what prompted me to ask, "Will Yolanda be there?"

After a moment of silence he said, "It's at her place."

"I don't have jack to say to you, just that maybe I need you to be in *my corner*. Do you know what I mean?"

He had the nerve to sound amused. "You have such a way with words."

"So, are you saying that I am invited?"

". . . to the party?" he said for me before answering. "No." It is just a small thing. His mischievous tone pissed me off. "I'll have something very special waiting for you when you get home." Was he changing the subject? Who needed this shit, especially on the heels of one of the most significant days of trial? Breanna was scheduled to testify tomorrow. If I didn't go for a jog, I was going to kill somebody. "Craig, I think that we have taken this merry go round as far as we can. I'm jumping off."

"Jumping where?" He actually sounded surprised. "How about I give you a call later?"

"For what? I can't keep pretending that everything is okay with me in this thing." The reality that I had put up with enough hit me hard, and left me cold. Underneath the pain, though, was a good feeling like I'd hit the lottery. I tore off my clothes and grabbed my running shorts while I listened to Craig.

"Spiegel," he said. His voice was calm but cold. "We are not married and Yolanda is a friend."

'We are not married' ran through my mind like credits at the end of a movie.

Silenced. My mouth was opened but nothing came out. I froze while lacing up my sneakers. The riveting plush green hills of Bermuda called out.

"Okay?" he asked cautiously. "So, I'll call you later?"

"Craig, unless you plan on doing something about anything I've said please stay away from me."

"But . . . don't you think we should talk?"

Click.

Chapter Twenty-Two

Breanna stepped up to place her hand on the Bible before taking the witness stand. She wore her mother's gold love-knot necklace with a laced collar, cream cotton blouse. Her make-up looked natural, conservative, yet serene. The skirt she picked to go with the blouse was a pink, cream, and white floral print. She looked the part she was trying to play—a young, innocent naïve girl who'd made a mistake.

"I do swear to tell the truth, Your Lordship," she answered before the question was even asked. Her voice trembled.

God and my right hand, read the plaque above Lordship Appleby's chair. "You may be seated." She was so nervous that her butt almost missed the seat. Her day on the hot seat was finally here.

I rose and took a gulp of water, clutched my notes, and walked slowly, deliberately, toward Breanna. "Would you like some water, Breanna?" I asked.

"Yes. Thank you." She was fidgety, anxious. The water, the act of doing something else, I thought, would calm her. It did not.

"Are you all right?"

"Yes." She rubbed her small hands together and looked up at me tenderly.

"Please tell the court your name."

"My name is Breanna Jordan."

"How old are you, Breanna?"

"I am twenty-six."

James, who had been quietly sitting in the courtroom got up and left. He looked more afraid than Breanna—and I didn't even think that that was possible. Everyone was very quiet.

I continued, "Please tell us, would you please, Breanna, how did you come to know Sean Thomas?"

"We met at a party for a friend."

"Where did you go to college?"

"Syracuse University."

"And, what did you study?"

"Journalism, —"

I interrupted her. I wanted the jury to see her aspirations. "Please tell us again, how did you meet Sean?"

"He was parking cars at a fundraiser for my dad."

"He worked for your father?"

"No, he worked at the hotel where my daddy was having an event."

"Did he attend the event?"

"He wasn't supposed to be there, but later he did come into the party. I was dancing and he kept tapping me on my waist and ducking behind people so I wouldn't know who was hitting me."

"Did he eventually get your attention?"

She raised her perfectly arched bows. "Yes."

"And, when was that—what year?"

"That was 1996."

"Your Lordship, I'd like to introduce Defendant's Exhibit No. 13, a chronological chart of the relationship between Breanna and Sean Thomas."

Lordship Appleby looked over at the prosecution's table. No objection to the exhibit.

"May I have a copy?" Perry asked promptly.

I handed it to Appleby and gave Perry a smaller version of the blown-up chronology.

"Did he ask you out?"

Dirk sat in her direct line of vision. "Yes." She looked at Dirk. It kept her calm. By now, James had returned and walked swiftly to his seat next to Dirk.

"Do you recall your first date?"

"It was shortly after we met; maybe a few days."

I walked over to the graphic and uncovered the text. On the way over, a cell phone went off and laughter circulated in the courtroom. Lordship Appleby looked sternly at a journalist rushing from the courtroom, clutching the phone.

"Did you date Sean the entire time?"

"I'm not sure what you mean." Her voice was steady. Her hands stayed in her lap.

"Did you date him every day during those three years?"

"We broke up once."

"Do you recall when that was?"

"About a year ago."

"Would that be 1999?"

"I think . . . 1998." She corrected me.

"And why did you break up?"

"Because I caught him with another woman in my apartment, in my bedroom." The jury stirred uneasily.

"What did you do when you found him in your bed with someone else?"

"I was so upset that I ran out."

"You left your own apartment?"

She was doing okay so far. "Yes."

"Did you have words with Sean or anyone else at the time?"

"No. I was just so upset that I ran to my brother's house."

190 / GAIL RAMSEY

"And then what happened?"

"We talked and made up."

Sean's family erupted with whispers and gestures. Breanna jerked around in their direction, startled by the sudden chatter.

"Sean said that he was trying to let his fiancée down easy."

"He told you that the relationship with his fiancée was over?"

"Objection!" Perry yelled so loud that Breanna jumped. She looked at Perry then to Lordship Appleby before returning her attention to me.

"Sustained. Rephrase," Appleby ruled.

"You understood that the relationship between the deceased and Ms. Fay Summer was over?"

"Yes!" Breanna stiffened her spine and sat up straight. It almost looked as though she placed her hand on her hips before returning them to her lap. I hoped Perry did not notice that the mere mentioning of Fay's name sent Breanna into a tailspin.

"Breanna, did you love Sean?"

"Yes. I loved him very much." She did not cry out as the tears rolled down her cheeks. "And I would never hurt him."

"What were you thinking when you sped off on your moped?"

"I just wanted to get away." She lowered her head and the long phony ponytail fell to the side of her face. "I never meant to hurt Sean."

"Just one more question."

"When did you learn that the relationship between Sean and his fiancée was not in fact over?"

"He never told me."

"Thank you, Breanna. No further questions, Your Lordship."

Breanna sat. It was hard for *me* to read her, let alone a jury. I watched them as I moved from the podium to take my seat. They looked somber. Their gazes still lingered on Breanna as Perry stood to address her.

A murmur in the courtroom came from the press.

"Ms. Jordan, do you need to take a break?" Lordship Appleby was being considerate as he waved his hand at Perry to stand in place.

"Yes, Your Honor, I mean Your Lordship," she said in a childlike tone.

"The Court will take a twenty-minute break." The jury was escorted out of sight and we pretty much stood in place, encouraging Breanna to keep her chin up. She had done well.

I walked out on the lawn to get some air. James followed me.

We stood on the well-kept grounds overlooking the grassy sunlit terrain. The grass parted along the stone walkways leading up to the big white courthouse.

"Did you give any more thought to what I said to you the other night?"

"When is Charli due?" It felt good to say her name.

"I just took her to the airport," he said. Was I supposed to be happy? "Can I take you to dinner tonight?" What about karma?

"Not now, James." I was otherwise quiet but said, "It's time to get back upstairs."

"Spiegel . . ." James waved his hands but no words came out of his mouth.

"What is it?" James' timing was always off.

"Charli married me to have a baby."

"Are you saying you were just genetic material?"

"You are so sarcastic."

"James, really. Your wife is twenty-two years old. She has damn near a lifetime to have babies." I was the one up against a ticking biological clock.

"She's gay, Spiegel."

"James, you're lying. I don't believe you, and even if I did, you married her."

"She is, you know what I'm trying to say, Spiegel." He paused. "I didn't know when I married her."

"No. I don't know what you are talking about."

"This is not coming out right. I'd rather talk about us. I don't love her. I love you."

Watch what you invite into your life; shit didn't just happen, it multiplied, had become my silent motto. "You loved her at one time or thought you did."

"I was confused." He scratched the top of his head. *And you're still confused.*

"We better get upstairs, James. This trial is not over."

Perry was just getting started when James and I reentered the courtroom. Breanna had just sat down and the jury members were being escorted back into their seats.

Perry stood to address her. "Did you kill Sean Thomas?" Perry charged out of the gate.

"No, Mr. Perry. I mean, Sean is dead and I caused it, but I didn't mean to cause his death." She was talking too much.

"Did you ram a bike into Mr. Thomas?"

"Objection."

"On what grounds?" Perry snapped back.

"Overruled. You may answer."

She nodded again.

"You must answer verbally. The court reporter cannot record gestures," said Appleby.

"Yes." She played with the hem of her skirt.

"Why, if you knew you may have caused injury to someone, why did you leave the island?"

"I didn't know that he was hurt. I thought that he would catch a taxi and come back to the hotel."

"Why, did he scream out to you that he was going to take a taxi?"

"Objection."

"Overruled."

"No."

Lordship Appleby cautioned Breanna to pause for his ruling before answering.

"Did he yell out to you, 'Please stop; help me'?"

"No."

"No, because he *could* not."

"Objection."

"Sustained. The jury will disregard the commentary. Mr. Perry, let me caution you to save your summary of the case for your closing."

"Ms. Jordan," he said, his voice escalated to its highest pitch, "is it true that the entire time you dated Sean Thomas, he was engaged to another woman?"

"He said that the engagement was off."

"Isn't it a fact that he ended his affair with you twice to return to his fiancée?"

"No."

"No? How long have you dated Sean Thomas?"

"Objection. Asked and answered."

"Overruled," ruled Appleby.

"Three years."

"And, how many times during that period did you end your relationship?"

"Once, maybe twice."

"And, each time did he tell you that he was working things out with his fiancée?"

"No."

"Did you love Sean Thomas?"

"Yes, I thought I did."

"You *thought* you did?"

"Yes," Breanna answered.

"Do you think differently today?"

"No. I love him today. I still do."

"Is that why you killed him?"

"Objection."

"Sustained. Mr. Perry, rephrase the question."

"Did you get mad when you learned that Sean was ending your relationship with you to marry his fiancée?"

"Sean wasn't leaving me."

"Isn't it true that you got so mad that you drove a bike right smack into him, causing him to fall to his death?"

"I didn't mean for Sean to die." The tears welling in her eyes fell one by one down her face. She wiped them away gently with the palm of her hands.

"Sean did not want you."

"Objection."

"Overruled."

Breanna was red. She was rocking back and forth in the chair. "He *did* want me."

"You wanted to kill Sean, didn't you?" He screamed loudly in Breanna's face.

"Your Honor." I stood.

"You bastard!" Breanna yelled. "You don't know. I just ran."

"You ran and Sean Thomas died. No further questions, Your Lordship."

Felix sat, tortured, looking at Breanna. He had taken time off for the trial and had sat through all the sordid details of the troubled life of his little girl—the details sprung forth at each stage of the trial. But, when Breanna took the stand he developed a nervous twitch, and it was getting worse. Breanna had had her day in court.

Lordship Appleby announced, "Closing arguments will begin a week from Thursday at eight o'clock; afterwards the jury will render its verdict. Court is adjourned."

Chapter Twenty-Three

With the week off from court, I went back to Philly. It felt good to wake up in my own bed, looking over at the Bible stationed on the nightstand. What would life be like if I had time to pray and meditate? I dressed quickly and was out the door in a flash to a doctor's appointment.

The words Hematology-Oncology Department boldly met me at the door. I held my breath. Aliá had promised to meet me. Where was she? I sat and tried to relax behind the pages of *My Soul to Keep*. I avoided making eye contact with anyone, pretending to be reading my novel until someone pointed out that my book was upside down.

"Spiegel Cullen?" The plump, middle-aged receptionist announced that the doctor was ready to see me. Aliá caught up with me in time to sit down with the doctor as did my mother.

"Spiegel, hello," said the doctor.

"This is my mom, June, and my little sister Aliá."

"Sister . . . why you always say little sister?" Aliá spat.

Dr. Kline looked demure. *Something* was written all over his face, but I could not figure out what that was until he escorted us into a consultation room nicely decorated with departmental awards. "This is not what you see on TV about people with leukemia," he said once we were seated. He didn't waste time. "There is good news and bad news."

"Leukemia?" I questioned. Aliá gasped.

"What does that mean?" Mom asked calmly.

"Leukemia?" I whispered.

We all looked at him, puzzled.

"The good news—your blood tests shows a chronic leukemia, which can be very slow moving. I've been monitoring one patient for seventeen years."

He called that good news. "Am I going to die?" I looked over at Aliá; she was pale, and that was rare.

"We are all going to die," Dr. Kline answered. "The bad news is that there is no cure for leukemia."

"Disease?" I questioned. "Are you saying that I have a disease?" It seemed like a bad dream. I could not believe that I was sitting there.

"Spiegel," the doctor turned to me, "this is in a very early stage. We'll have to keep an eye on you over the next few months to see if there is any change."

"Where did this come from?" I asked.

"We don't know." He shrugged. "We think perhaps a virus."

"Can you cure it?" I asked. "Oh, that's right, you said there is no cure. What do I do?" I was falling apart.

"We do nothing for now."

"Excuse me."

"The only thing that I see is an elevation in the white cells. You are fine now. Why don't I have the nurse run another blood test today to confirm the initial test results? Surprisingly, all of your other cell counts were very good."

Aliá stood and raised her hands. "Wait. You just told her she has leukemia. What do you mean there is nothing wrong?"

"We don't usually see this particular chronic form of leukemia in people your age. It is rare." He emphasized rare.

Aliá left the room with tears streaming down her face. As she passed me, she sucked her teeth and rolled her eyes and said, "We're going for another opinion." She left the room abruptly. She would never in a million years be able to handle it if anything were to happen to me. She was probably pretending like we were not here, and that the doctor was not saying what I couldn't believe was coming out of his mouth myself. Why me?

Silence.

"What is the treatment?" My mom asked Dr. Kline.

"The truth of the matter is, Spiegel can outlive most of us." What was he really saying?

"What is the treatment?" my mom asked again.

"We can treat this leukemia with chemo if things get progressively worse." He glanced down at his notes.

"Cancer? Leukemia is cancer?" I asked loudly.

"Yes. The chemotherapy, in most cases, will trigger a remission in some chronic types of leukemia."

"Chemotherapy?"

The doctor looked up as Aliá entered the room again. "It is tolerated very well by most people," Dr. Kline continued.

Aliá dried her eyes. "Will my sister lose her hair?"

More silence.

"Will she lose her hair?" Aliá asked again. My girl. I could always count on her to ask the questions I was too scared to face.

"No." This doctor was giving me a bunch of crap everyone knew cancer, chemotherapy, hair loss. What the hell was I going to do? Where were the cameras that came in and said, "Smile, you're on a hidden camera?" What a cruel trick. Why me?

"Never," I heard myself say. "When will I have to do this?"

"Again, we have to wait and see. We want to run another test to confirm one way or the other." He paused. "I should say that I don't want to be too quick to diagnose without further tests. You are very young."

"So do I just walk out of here, no prescription, nothing?"

"If you need to call me for anything," he said, "do so. Otherwise, we will see you in three months."

"Aren't the white cells good for fighting cold germs?" I had entered my direct examination mode.

"Yes, but in cases of leukemia, the white blood cells are abnormally formed, therefore they don't perform as well. "

He made it sound so easy. "What about kids?" I said before I had a chance to decide not to say it out loud.

"What about kids?" The doctor returned the question to me. The doctor was smooth. I liked him immediately, I just didn't appreciate his conversation.

"Are you trying to tell us something, Spiegel?" my mother asked.

"No." She was annoying me. "Will this prevent me from having children?"

He flipped hastily through my records. "Are you married?"

"No."

"Well, first things first: find a nice guy," he joked. Everyone, including Aliá, laughed nervously.

"Are there any other questions?" he asked, and stood promptly to respond to a knock at the door. He bid us farewell and was off.

"Let's get out of here. I'm starving," I said.

"I'm not very hungry," said my mother. She probably wanted to go somewhere alone and pray. She hugged me. It felt good until she said, "Why don't you allow yourself to be happy, baby? Where is your joy?"

I had cancer and she was talking about "where is your joy."

"Easy for you to say, Mom."

"Oh no, honey. It is not easy for me to say. I love you, baby. But, you are not going to die today. You heard the doctor."

"No, I am," Aliá said, with her hands firmly on her hips, "if we don't get out of this place." We moved through a packed waiting room to take the elevator to the parking garage.

We walked Mom to her customized black Range Rover. My dad calls it her play car. She hugged me again—hugged me tightly.

"I'm okay, Mom." I tried to reassure her.

"I know you are." She needed no reassurance.

"I'll call you later."

We stood and watched her drive off before getting into my car. "Ah, it might be time for you to get some new wheels," Aliá huffed. "I have the rest of the day off and I want you to go somewhere with me, be nice to go in style!" Aliá continued as she fastened her seat belt.

"Shoot!" I yelled when I remembered that I'd forgotten to stop at the nurses' station to give more blood.

"What?"

"I forgot to give more blood."

"No worries," Aliá said in her newly acquired British accent, "I gave for you."

"You did what?" I stopped short of putting the key in the ignition.

"I told them that I was Spiegel Cullen when I left the room for a second. Now, we'll see if the doctor is a quack." She laughed.

"Where do you want to go?" I said, thinking I'd call the doctor later.

"I'll give you a clue, two words: maintenance man."

"What!"

"Come on, Spi. All this talk about cancer is stressing me out. We need *Tommy therapy*."

"You are serious, aren't you? Who?"

"I was going to see him anyway. Tommy can do you and his partner Curtis can do me."

"What you talking about, Aliá?"

"Smack Bottom Spa right on the corner of 24th & Fairmont. You will love them."

I then remembered her telling me about *Tommy Tom* as she called him, her masseuse.

"Can we at least eat first?"

"Puh-leez. We can grab a pretzel."

"Okay, now I know that you have lost your mind and you are taking me with you." I felt a surge of energy and tried to put my fears about the cancer aside. Aliá couldn't handle it if I fell apart.

"Are you going to tell Craig?" she asked. I knew she was worried but tried not to show it.

"Not! Anyway, he's history."

"Yes! You finally let go!" In some ways Aliá was like the big sister. She was so level headed when it came to guys especially. Ahmir adored her and she wouldn't accept anything less, but if I asked her about Ahmir right now she might say, "Ahmir who?" She was too busy smiling, anticipating the touch of her maintenance man.

Tommy and Curtis had converted a three-story brownstone into the most talked about spa in the city. Their specialty was having two people on you at the same time. Tommy greeted us doused in some natural outdoors-smelling cologne that was a cross between sweet and musk. It was pleasant and so was he. He escorted us both to a large massage room on the top floor. Two full-body tables were in the middle of a room painted various shades of ocean blue.

He asked us to fully undress and showed us where we could hang our clothes behind the door. Aliá smiled. "Are you doing us both in this room?"

He nodded. "Please lay face up on your back when you are ready," he said as he left the room.

A few minutes later he reentered with Curtis close behind him. We lay quietly face up.

A faint scent of honeysuckle rose filled the room from the scented candles Tommy had lit around the room. He dimmed the lights. I relaxed and closed my eyes to the tunes of water falling over a babbling creek. Tommy stood at the top of the table and gently massaged my face and temples. He later maneuvered to the side of the table and took out one side of my body, leaving the other half tucked under the cotton sheet. He spread my legs wider apart and stroked my inner thighs in wide circles. I could feel the heat between my legs and prayed that I wouldn't leave a wet spot. Tommy worked the fears away. I was hot and became more and more relaxed with every stroke and thought that Aliá, who was by now out cold, really knew what she was talking about.

"Bottoms up," Tommy commanded. He wanted me to turn over on my stomach. I did.

Curtis stood on one side while Tommy hovered on the other. While one leaned in with his whole body, I inhaled. He mashed and dragged his hands and finger down the lengthen of my back while the other one rubbed my toes, feet, calves, and thighs right on up to the curves of my gluteus maximus. I felt like I was going to explode and prayed even more that they would understand about the wet spot.

As I heard Curtis tell Aliá to turn over, I realized that his hands had left my body. I felt that I'd left my body as well—died and gone to heaven. I'd never in my life felt so relaxed. I lay on the table as Tommy covered my backside and moved his magic fingers to my neck and head.

I dozed off and didn't wake until Tommy tapped me on the shoulders, and asked, "Do you need to get that?" My cell phone was ringing.

"Damn." The cell phone interrupted the flow.

Aliá reached for the telephone. "Mom, can I call you right back? Yes, she is here. We will call you back in a few minutes."

"Our mother," Aliá said.

"Are you satisfied?" Tommy asked before turning off the babbling brooks and flicking on the lights.

I could only nod, and Aliá smiled a mischievous I-told-you-so smile.

When we left the spa, I felt like I was twenty-two, young, and carefree. I vowed to come back as I hugged Tommy and Curtis good-bye.

"What did Mom want?" I asked as we strolled lightheartedly to the car.

"She wants you to start drinking wheat-grass juice." We both laughed hysterically on the way home.

Chapter Twenty-Four

From Philadelphia back to Bermuda, I poured my heart and soul into preparing for my closing remarks. The final day of trial commenced on the third Monday in April.

Kevin Perry had shown off his skill and experience as a prosecutor. He hammered away at each of the witnesses called to testify in the case against Breanna. Admittedly, Sean was dead; but it was an accident. I had to make the jury understand.

I had reached my boiling point with Perry's closing comments: "There is nothing any of us can do to bring him back, but what you, the jury, can do is to bring his murderer to justice. Don't close your eyes."

This was it. "Good morning." I stood quickly to compose myself. "It's customary to thank you, the jury, at this point, and I do sincerely. We still have one final step, and the clock continues to tick. How will you decide? Your job has not been easy, listening to all of the evidence, deciding what to believe, deciding who is telling the truth. It is a hard job, and a very important one, because a woman's life is in your hands."

The jurors were becoming clearer to me now. Their expressions were intent. Mrs. Wiggins was sitting on the edge of her seat.

"Breanna Jordan loved Sean Thomas, even though he lied to her, cheated on her, and manipulated her. Breanna loved Sean Thomas." When I walked from side to side, their gazes followed me.

I continued, "Nothing presented in this courtroom over the past weeks is enough to remove the doubts we have about what really happened to Sean Thomas on that fateful night." I paused.

"Does it make sense that a young couple vacationing on the beautiful island of Bermuda would end their stay in murder? I think not. Does it make sense to you that a girl who has her whole life before her would toss it to the wind? I think not."

"As much as this trial is about Breanna, it is about choices." My throat was closing up. I walked back to the counsel table, poured a glass of water, took a big gulp, and swallowed before moving on.

"I heard it said once that those split-second choices are the only ones that really matter. Breanna made a choice to speed off on her scooter, accidentally bumping Sean Thomas as she sped off. It was a mistake, yes. It was an accident, yes. It was a wrong choice, yes." I paused. "It was *not* murder."

"We have shown you the evidence; you have heard it from Breanna's own mouth. This was a relationship in trouble from the beginning. Yet, in spite of the lies, Breanna loved Sean." I had warmed up now.

"Breanna left Bermuda thinking that Sean was somewhere close behind her. She left Bermuda with a broken heart. She was not fleeing justice. She had no reason to believe she had done anything wrong. Perhaps naïve. Perhaps a bad choice. But not murder. She felt extremely betrayed and frustrated and rejected, as we all may have felt at some point in our own lives. But we don't kill, and neither did she."

"His Lordship will tell you when you deliberate that proof is based on the evidence presented *solely* during the trial. There is no evidence that shows Breanna intended to lure Sean to

Bermuda to kill him. This is not murder. They were vacationing, having a good time."

I walked over to my yellow pad to make sure I had covered everything. I gave a quick summary of each witness called to testify on Breanna's behalf, each detail of Breanna's emotional breakdown when she learned of Sean's death, how the death of her mother affected her, and her sensitive, naïve nature. She was like a paper doll being played by a puppeteer.

I repeated my crescendo one last time before I took my seat at counsel table: "It was an accident. It was *not* murder."

After a short recess, Lordship Appleby charged the jury and sent them off to deliberate at ten minutes to eleven. Judgment day had come.

We gathered our papers and huddled.

The stress of the trial was starting to gel on Breanna's pretty face; she looked many years older than she had even a few weeks ago, let alone a year ago.

"What do you think, Spiegel?" Breanna asked.

Waiting for a jury was like getting a tooth pulled without anesthesia. "We wait."

"I want to thank you, Spiegel." Had reality finally smacked her in the face? "Whatever happens, thank you."

On the brink of an emotional breakdown myself, I was fighting back tears. It warmed my spirit to think that I was helping someone. But, I was struggling at that moment to appear strong, in control. "You are welcome."

I kept fumbling with my papers while she continued to look at me. If she were found guilty, I'd appeal. I would continue to search for evidence to free Breanna. I was ashamed to admit that I didn't believe her at first.

I wanted desperately to focus on the positive—that maybe the jury saw the good in Breanna, that maybe the doctors were wrong about my cancer. It was becoming increasingly difficult to imagine Breanna deliberately shoving Sean off the cliff and equally difficult to see me with a disease. I forced myself to think only about the moment. If she walked, she was one lucky girl. The jury was too hard to read.

I was done. The trial was over and I was worried. My experience had taught me the longer the jury was out the better the chances of an acquittal. I was juggling with lady optimism.

"Where is Dirk?" I asked Stephen. He was noticeably absent.

"I dunno."

Felix held Breanna. I left the courtroom alone. James followed me.

We jumped into a taxi to the hotel.

In the past weeks, the hotel suite had been converted to an office and had crackled with arguments and endless conversations. We now sat quietly amidst the packed boxes as the hotel staff assembled the assorted veggies and hot pasta for lunch along with cookies, cakes, teas, and coffees. Ola scurried about packing our cargo for Philly.

I left the suite. James followed me.

Behind the closed doors of my room, James spoke first. "Please let me—"

I felt the warmth of his breath gently on my cheek. I needed him. I longed to be wrapped in the arms of someone who loved me; someone who'd rub my back and make life fair again.

He held me so close, so tight for so long, I shook.

I'd surely be damned for wanting James. "Do you have protection?"

"Why? Do I need it?" James said in one breath. He scratched the top of his head.

"You have a wife," I replied. My words shook me to the core. "You have a wife," I said again.

James kissed me softly to quell my mumbling and he squeezed me tightly when I returned his passion. I wanted him to hold me; I wanted him to tell me how much he loved me, how much he wanted me, how much he'd missed me. We all have those defining moments in our lives; those single moments that can change a life forever. My moment was here.

James and I did a smooth two-step before landing on the bed. I looked deeply into his puppy dog eyes. We didn't speak. We didn't have too. In his eyes, I saw nothing—no pictures of tomorrow or the next day. I lay with him—but not really with him. He had a wife and babies now. We held each other until sleep came. My dance with the devil was done.

Only a few minutes after our heads hit the pillow, I got the call that the jury had reached a verdict.

The courtroom was packed by the time we returned. The spectators' section was standing room only. All of the major newspapers from London, the United States, and Bermuda were there, as were most of the television stations. This was the biggest thing that had hit Bermuda since the Bermuda Triangle. This case was its own sort of triangle, and just as deadly.

James held Breanna's hand, leading her up to the counsel table, just as he did at their mother's funeral. The brother and sister looked like twins, clad in fear and anguish.

Sean Thomas' family and friends were present and noisy.

Aliá was supposed to come in that morning, but she must have been detained. I missed my sister, and wished that I could look up and see her face.

The jury box was filling as spectators fiercely scrambled for any remaining seats. My heart pounded as Lordship Appleby asked, "Mrs. Wiggins, has the jury reached a verdict?"

"Yes, we have, Your Lordship, sir."

Breanna and I eased up from our chairs. We didn't dare move, not even to swat a fly circling around us as we stood at counsel table, facing Lordship Appleby. I felt a light tap on my right shoulder and turned to see Ola standing behind me.

I frowned and whispered sternly, "Have you lost your mind?" I frowned harder and whispered deeper, "What?"

"Spiegel. Your sister has been in an accident."

I turned around to face Ola. Appleby looked over at the jury but cocked his head in our direction. "Is she all right?" I continued to whisper. Ola did not answer. She motioned for me to follow her and stepped away. "Give me a minute," I said. Was Aliá hurt?

All eyes rested on the jurors as Appleby spoke to them. "What say you, guilty or not guilty, on the charge of murder in the first degree?"

"Not guilty, Your Lordship." A breeze of relief rushed through the defense table.

Shout outs filled the courtroom from the family of Sean Thomas. "Good Lord, No! No!"

"On the lesser charge murder in the second degree, what is your verdict, guilty or not guilty?"

My heart was pounding so hard that I trembled. This time the jury foreman looked in Breanna's direction before saying, "We find the defendant not guilty, Your Lordship."

Yes! I thought and looked over my shoulder at Ola. By now, she was in the back of the room pacing.

"As to the charge, involuntary manslaughter, guilty or not guilty?"

"Guilty, Your Lordship."

"Fuck!" I said, softly but hard. The jury saw it as a killing of passion.

"She's innocent!" cried Breanna's family and friends, while the family of Sean Thomas did everything to keep from jumping up and down perceiving some sense of justice. Lordship Appleby tapped his gavel.

Breanna buried her head in her father's chest. James' cries were heard above everyone else. He ran to his father and Breanna and embraced them. James looked almost as bad as he did when he tracked me down to take the case.

Suddenly, Dirk rushed into the courtroom waiving papers to get our attention. He ran immediately to Walter, motioning for the lawyers to come before Lordship Appleby.

"It is all here!" he yelled, reaching Walter at the counsel table.

Ola was still standing nervously now next to me, nudging me to leave.

"Your Lordship," Walter said. "We have new information that has direct bearing on the outcome of this case."

The chaotic chatter and moving about in the courtroom came to an immediate hush.

Kevin Perry was on his feet. "The case is *over!*" he yelled. "I don't understand."

"Your Lordship. We have evidence that someone else was on the beach that night, struggled with Sean, and killed him," Walter said. "We have photographs, Your Lordship."

"You are lying! You are a liar," came from the back of the courtroom. "She killed him. She killed him. I *saw* them." Everyone turned in the direction of the screams.

"I saw them," Fay said as she crumbled to the floor. "I saw them there on the beach . . . loving. He promised me, but I saw them." She sobbed.

Lordship Appleby tapped his gravel repeatedly until the courtroom was silent. He dismissed the jury, ordered the guards to take Fay Summer into custody, and asked the barristers to meet in his chambers.

"Court is adjourned" were the words I heard as I fled the courtroom dodging the cameras and reporters. Ola was in the hall, holding some of my personal items and an airline ticket. She escorted me briskly through the hall to a waiting cab for the trip to the airport.

The flight back to Philly felt endless. Looking at my Dad's sullen face when the plane touched down, confirmed that something was seriously wrong.

"What is it, Dad?" He greeted me at the airport. He hugged me so tightly I could hardly catch my breath. Sheer panic filled me.

"Dad?"

"Your mom's at the hospital now."

"What happened?"

"It is horrible, Spiegel. Aliá is in a coma."

"Woo!" I gasped. "She'll be all right." Of course, I had no way of knowing that, but I knew that Aliá had to be okay, no matter what. "A coma?"

"They are watching her, but it does not look good."

I grabbed Dad and didn't want to let go. The people at the airport were looking at us. "Let's go, Dad," I said.

"Do you have luggage?"

"No." Ola rushed me out so quickly.

Dad was crying. He walked bent over. He was devastated. His baby girl. My heart went out to him. I had to be strong.

"She will be okay, Dad."

"It doesn't look good, Spiegel." I refused to believe it.

"What happened?"

"A pier collapsed."

"What! A what?"

"One of those piers down there on the waterfront." Was Dad hysterical?

"Were they walking on a pier?"

"No. It was on one of those piers that have a restaurant or something. She was there with her girlfriends, having dinner."

"It was open for business?" I asked.

Silence. He shook his head in anger.

By the time I'd reached my mom, I nearly passed out. I rushed to her. "Oo-ooh Lord. What is it?"

Mom hugged me tightly. Ahmir walked in a small circle hitting his right fist in his left hand. My Dad was speaking with the doctor, and a little old nun lady.

"We do not think that she is going to make it," said the doctor.

"God No! Mom, please! Please! Aliá! Aliá!" My words were unsteady. I didn't remember falling to the floor when Ahmir and the little old lady helped me to my feet. I was making sounds but the words were not forming correctly. I walked down a long corridor to see Aliá. I'll make her laugh—I began to bargain with God.

The lights in the room were low. Aliá lay covered in a sheet up to her neck. It really was her lying there, still. A young doctor stood by her side.

"Doctor, what's wrong with her? Will she be okay?"

"She is in bad shape." His words were cold, empty on emotion.

Aliá. The wires sprawled out on top of her bedspread but she was not plugged up to anything. "Plug her up!" I yelled. "Plug my sister back into that machine or I'll—! Please, put it back together."

Ahmir walked past some of my aunts, who were now present, to hug me. He rocked me. I'd never seen such beautiful, strong black men and women look so defeated. "I love her, Spiegel." His eyes were swollen and red.

"She's okay now, Spiegel. God will carry your sister." The little nun lady didn't know what to say. If she wasn't out of my sight in two minutes I was going to smack the living shit out of her.

"Shut up!" I screamed. "I want my sister! I touched Aliá's face. She was warm, but I felt a chill as though my face had been brushed by a spider-web when I kissed her cheek. "Liá!" I called her name, trying to wake her up the way I used to do when we were kids.

She just lay there.

I was losing it. "Doctor, please."

"We are doing all that we can." The doctor tried to console me.

We huddled—Mom, Dad, Ahmir, and me. We huddled and did the only thing we knew to do. We prayed.

Chapter Twenty-Five

The next several days passed in a blur. The Mother's Day race was here again and Aliá was still in a coma. The doctors were cautiously optimistic about her condition. She had undergone two surgeries to reduce swelling of her brain. Now, they said, we had to wait and see.

I shut my eyes tightly for a full minute and willed my mind to stop churning then I began suiting up for the race. It had started to rain, but not hard enough to cancel the race. More runners than I'd ever seen had gathered by the time I arrived.

No sooner had I wiggled through the crowd for the start of the race, when I took-in the most compassionate and strong set of familiar brown eyes. "Spiegel."

"Tyler." It was too late to hide the stream flowing from my eyes. I jumped. "What a surprise!" I wiped the tears still remaining on my cheeks. I cried every time I thought of Aliá and that was pretty much twenty-four seven. Had I'd known something so awful could have happened, I would have—.

"Are you okay?" he said, touching me on the shoulder.

"I guess I'm okay."

The professional man with the pony tail and diamond stud. "It is a pleasure seeing you again. Did you get my flowers?"

"Your flowers?"

"You didn't get them?" he asked.

I couldn't recall quick enough so I asked, "What are you doing here?" I felt nervous as if I was sixteen and kissing a boy for the very first time.

"I'm trying to stay fit like you . . . you know." He held up both arms like Hercules, showing off his muscles. He was fit, just as I had imagined under his usual attire. He was wearing black lycra running shorts and a *Race for the Cure* T-shirt. The shorts showed off every curve and bulge.

I tried not to be obvious, but he looked so well-endowed. "Nice," I said to the Hercules gesture, and we both laughed.

"Any change with Aliá?" We stopped laughing immediately.

"No."

"Is that your beeper?"

"Yes." I pulled it from my waist pack. I didn't recognize the number so I put it away.

As we ran together, I slowed down, purposely, to keep up with Tyler, who was running at a conversational pace, a slow jog. I liked it. "Are you going to run like this the whole race?" I asked.

"Sure. If you don't mind . . . every race doesn't have to be about finishing fast. Let me just enjoy your company and conversation." He was flirting with me. Nice.

Three weeks since the accident and it felt like yesterday. And all I'd done since was cry the blues. Walter had remained in Bermuda to handle the extradition hearing for Breanna so that I could stay in Philly. Breanna was busy hanging out with Dirk, but they had stopped by once to see Aliá before heading back to Bermuda.

Tyler brought my thoughts back to the moment by asking, "Are you still taking care of business for the Jordan family?"

We ran toe-to-toe as we talked. "No. All charges against Breanna were dropped."

"I heard," he said.

"I'm taking time out. We better speed up a little if we want to finish the race today."

We managed to keep to a nice trot throughout most of the race. A few minutes later, my beeper sounded again.

"What about the other young lady, the wife?"

"Fiancée. Guilty."

"Of murder?"

"Yeah. She could have gotten life."

". . . all things considered . . ." he finished my sentence.

"Dirk is a heck of an investigator. He found airline records that placed Fay in Bermuda, but what was even more ironic was that the taxi driver we were trying to track down was a bit of a voyeur. The police uncovered photographs of Fay and Sean at the beach that night."

"No!" Tyler flashed a grand smile.

"Yep. The photographs were the instant automatic kind and they were very intimate."

"You mean . . ."

"Yep."

We did a quick zig-zag around a jogger with a stroller.

"Fay said she saw them on the beach together." I took a deep breath. "She confessed to everything—the murder, the phone calls, even putting Sam up to coming after Breanna."

"Wow. I guess you do need time off with everything going on in your life."

I was opening up and felt flushed. "What have you been up to?" A lot of people sent get-well flowers to Aliá when they heard about the accident. But, Tyler, I recalled now, sent a dozen pink roses trimmed in red to me.

"I didn't hear from you, but was hoping that I would. I just bought some property over there so I've been busy with that."

"Bermuda?"

He nodded. "I was hoping you'd call. I felt—"

"I was going to call you but . . ." I wanted to say, *but I was too scared to call you, too scared to trust my heart.* "Thanks for the flowers." *Roses.*

We jogged for a time in silence. Squirrels playfully rustled the green leaves of the Slippery Elm trees, watching the joggers trot on by.

"Is that your beeper again?"

Once through the finish line, I reached for my cell phone from the granny pack to return the call.

"Did someone page Spiegel Cullen?"

"Yes. You are requested at the hospital as soon as possible."

"Who is this?"

"Your mom asked that I phone you immediately. She is in with your sister."

"Is my sister okay?"

"She wants to see you."

I leaped in the direction of my car, with Tyler following close behind me.

"Come this way," he said, gliding me in a different direction. "I'll drive you." I did as he asked. It felt good to let someone guide me.

We arrived at the hospital within minutes. I didn't even stop to get a visitor's pass and check-in. I darted up to the twenty-sixth floor to Aliá's room. Before I even got to her room, I heard lots of talking and what sounded like laughter. Laughter, and it was coming from the same room I had approached with such gloom for the past several days. That day, the joy would not be denied.

"Ohmygod!" She looked at me with tears rolling down her face.

"She is going to be fine, Spiegel," said my mother, who along with my father could hardly contain herself.

I ran to my sister. "Aliá!"

"Spiegel, my friends." She became agitated trying to tell me that she lost her best friend when the pier collapsed. I knew though. Dozens of people were injured and three people killed—one of them Sky Brown, one of Aliá's best friends. My mother sounded the buzzer for the nurse to give Aliá something to calm her.

"I know. I know." I held her close.

The nurse breezed into the room, to my surprise followed by Dr. Kline, the hematologist. Dr. Kline spoke first as the nurse cared for Aliá. "You Cullen sisters pulled a trick on me."

We were silent.

"Why are you here?" I asked.

"What are you talking about?" my mom asked.

"Was it the blood I gave for Spiegel?" Aliá asked.

"What we thought was a blood sample from your sister," Dr. Kline nodded toward Aliá, was genetically different enough so that we became alarmed and launched an investigation."

We hung on his every word.

The nurse left the room.

"What is going on?" My mother asked again.

Dr. Kline looked at me.

I felt embarrassed. "Dr. Kline I was going to call your office to re-do the blood but—"

"Spiegel, as it turned out, an inexperienced pathologist missed or misinterpreted some of the samples, leaving us with the inconclusive lab results." He paused. "Lots of false positives and otherwise faulty results."

"Do I have leukemia?"

"We don't think so."

"Thank you, Jesus," my mom whispered.

By now Aliá was fighting sleep.

I was in shock. I should have had a thousand questions but I couldn't think of one. I just stood there with my mouth open.

Dr. Kline smiled. My mother did a praise dance. I didn't know what to do.

I had lost all track of time and forgot that Tyler was with me. Three whole hours had passed since I first arrived. I kissed Aliá and told her that I was going home to change and would be back when she woke up later that afternoon.

"She woke up," I whispered.

Dr. Kline left, but not before he had me promise to visit his office. He said chronic fatigue syndrome could also cause similar symptoms.

I went out to the hall and pressed the button for the elevator. The bell sounded just as my mother called from the room, "Spiegel!" I stood frozen, watching my mother walk toward me. "*Liá* wants you to bring her something to eat."

I relaxed, overcome all of a sudden with a rush of emotions like rays of sunshine circling the rain. It was pure joy, no pain. "What does she want?"

"Fried chicken, collards, and real potatoes." We were goners. We wiped each other's tears but the tears kept falling. "Go," she said. "Liá can't eat anything like that yet. Oh no, honey. But as soon as my baby gets home, I'm a fix up all the collards greens, pickled beets, candy sweets, and real potatoes she can eat."

I took the elevator to the lobby. Tyler was waiting for me. He had changed into jeans fitted just enough to accent the curves of his tight ass. His diamond stud sparkled almost as bright as his smile. I loved his smile.

"I wanted to give you that time with Aliá. I went home to change."

"I see."

"Your sister is special." His voice was full of compassion.

"She's going to be okay, Tyler." I hugged him and, without calculating my next move, kissed him. "She's going to be okay."

"I'm here for you, Spiegel." He held onto me for a split second.

"Professionally speaking?" I asked.

"I was hoping personally. But, whatever." He paused. "Spiegel, is there something between you and James Jordan?"

"James?"

"Yes, I sensed . . . well I'm not sure what I sensed, but . . . "

"No." My thoughts drifted. "James is a friend." James was so sweet and supportive after the accident. He cooked a meal at my condo, he cleaned the kitchen, even took out the trash. But, we kept it real. In other words, we kept our clothes on. Whatever he had to work out with his wife didn't involve Spiegel Cullen. It was as if someone pulled the plug and James came out.

Tyler eyed me carefully. "We were talking about James."

"We were?"

"Have you seen the babies?"

"Babies . . . now, there's a dream deferred," I mumbled softly, or so I thought until I heard Tyler ask, "Excuse me?"

"Nothing."

"What is it?" He noticed the drift in my thoughts again. "Would you like to talk about it?"

"No." I meant yeah, but I said no. "Maybe later," I heard myself saying.

"Where are you?" he joked.

"Nothing. Why don't we stop for tea?" I light-heartedly said.

"At your service." He playfully bowed his head and extended his arm.

We waltzed into a Starbucks on the corner for lemon peppermint tea. We sat at a small round table near the window and blew on our tea to cool it.

"Let's toast," he said.

"To what?" I asked. I wanted to tell him about the leukemia, about the false positive, about how happy I felt inside.

"To better days ahead." He spoke my thoughts exactly. We clicked our cups.

"I was just wondering if James and his wife were your clients." I was being nosy. We sat our cups down, sipped, and talked.

"You know that would be confidential, but—no." He paused. "Is it James who has your heart?"

"No." Not anymore. I became in that instant aware of all the possibilities that exist in a moment.

He looked me in the eyes as though looking right through me. I felt naked. I tingled inside. I didn't turn away from his gaze until a sparkle around his neck caused me to blink.

"Who is Zen?" I asked.

"What do you mean?" He squinted.

"The name on your neck chain."

"Oh!" He laughed. His rich brown complexion oozed delightful reddish undertones as he shifted in his seat. He paused. "It is another way of saying exhaust the moment." He grabbed at the chain. "My reminder."

"Exhaust the moment?" I questioned.

"Haven't you heard of the Zen philosophy?"

I shook my head.

"It challenges you to step with the present and not worry about the past or future."

My mother's voice echoed in my ear, "You are alive today, Spiegel." "Interesting," was as much as I could say.

"A one-word response?" He was playing the shrink.

As I reflected on Tyler's words, I thought of embracing what was coming my way right now. "I get it though." A synergy of slow jams spiked with desire danced from him to me, and back again. "Make every moment count."

"Tick Tock."

Sug Books
An Imprint of

www.gailramsey.com